DEPTHS OF DANGER

The bullet exploded into the narrow tunnel, sending shards of rock flying from the ceiling, where it hit. Instantly there was a strange, muffled sound like thunder, and a tremor ripped through the mine's rock walls.

With a karate yell, Frank kicked at the weapon. Just as the gun flew into the darkness deeper inside the mine, an enormous piece of rock fell from the ceiling, landing inches from Frank.

Tiffany screamed, and Garth yanked her out of the way of the falling rocks. Frank wheeled around in time to see Joe dart to one side, narrowly missing being crushed.

Frank could no longer deny knowing what the sound rumbling louder and louder through the mine was.

"Get out—now!" he heard Garth yell. "The tunnel's collapsing!"

Books in THE HARDY BOYS CASEFILES® Series

Available from ARCHWAY Paperbacks

THE HARDY BOYS NO. 81

CASEFILES

SHEER TERROR

FRANKLIN W. DIXON

AN ARCHWAY PAPERBACK
Published by POCKET BOOKS
New York   London   Toronto   Sydney   Tokyo   Singapore

This book is a work of fiction. Names, characters, places and incidents are either products of the author's imagination or are used fictitiously. Any resemblance to actual events or locales or persons, living or dead, is entirely coincidental.

AN ARCHWAY PAPERBACK *Original*

An Archway Paperback published by
POCKET BOOKS, a division of Simon & Schuster Inc.
1230 Avenue of the Americas, New York, NY 10020

ISBN: 0-671-79465-5

First Archway Paperback printing November 1993

10 9 8 7 6 5 4 3 2 1

THE HARDY BOYS, AN ARCHWAY PAPERBACK and colophon are registered trademarks of Simon & Schuster Inc.

THE HARDY BOYS CASEFILES is a trademark of Simon & Schuster Inc.

Cover art by Brian Kotzky

Printed in the U.S.A.

IL 6+

Chapter

1

"MAIL CALL!" Joe Hardy shouted, bursting through the front door of his family's home and into the foyer. He waved a handful of envelopes in the air. "There's something for you, Aunt Gertrude—and a package for Dad."

"What about me?" Joe's older brother, Frank, appeared on the staircase in his workout clothes. "Callie said she'd write every day that she's at that choral competition."

"Be patient, Frank," Aunt Gertrude admonished, entering from the kitchen and plucking from Joe's hand the pale blue envelope that he had extended to her. "Callie and Vanessa just left two days ago. You boys won't hear from your girlfriends before Friday."

1

"Dad, you're the lucky one," Joe said as Fenton Hardy joined them in the now-crowded entryway. Joe tossed the package to his father. "This came special delivery. Maybe it's a Thanksgiving turkey."

"Far too light," Fenton remarked. Then his face broke into a smile. "It's from Sam Gentle," he said.

"Gentle?" Frank jogged the rest of the way downstairs. "I remember that name. Isn't he the scientist we visited when we were kids?"

"You mean the one with the really pesky daughter?" Joe set the rest of the mail on the foyer table. "The guy who worked for a chemical company?"

"That's right, and I seem to recall that you were pretty pesky yourself back then," Aunt Gertrude said with a sniff. "Tiffany's your age, Joe—seventeen. If she's as smart and pretty as her mother was, you might sing a different tune today."

Ignoring Frank's easy grin, Joe said to his father, "Open the package and show us what you got."

Fenton took a penknife from his pocket and carefully cut the package open. Plastic foam packing peanuts flew in all directions. Peering over his father's shoulder, Joe could see that the packing material cushioned a second, smaller box and a sealed envelope.

"You open the box," Fenton said, handing it to Gertrude. "I'll read the letter."

His curiosity aroused, Joe watched impatiently as his aunt lifted out a small clay pot several inches high. The pot had been broken and was pieced back together with the cracks and some holes showing. One side of it was charred, as if it had been in a fire.

"Let me guess," Joe said with a grin. "Dr. Gentle's taken up ceramics, but he left this one in the kiln too long."

"It looks old," Frank said, moving closer to inspect the pot. "Like something from an archaeological dig."

"I think you're right, Frank," Aunt Gertrude said. "See the white zigzag pattern? This must be one of Dr. Gentle's Anasazi relics."

"Anna who?" Joe asked.

"Sam Gentle had an extraordinary collection of Native American artifacts," Aunt Gertrude explained. "You're too young to remember them, probably, but I recall most of them and almost every word he said about them. Anasazi means 'the ancient ones.' Starting more than a thousand years ago, the Anasazi built great pueblo cities in what is now New Mexico and Arizona and southern Colorado. Then, around 1500, the tribes just disappeared. No one is sure what happened to them. We visited some of the ruins when we were out there."

3

"How would Dr. Gentle get his hands on something like this?" Joe asked, studying the pot.

Fenton looked up from the letter he was reading. "Sam's an amateur archaeologist," he said. "He wrote a book several years back about the petroglyphs found near some of the ancient ruins."

"What are petroglyphs?" Joe asked.

"They're drawings scratched or carved into the surface of cliffs and rocks," Frank told him. "I remember the Anasazi petroglyphs from our visit. They were stick figures, animals, spirals, zigzag lines, and other shapes. Scientists believe they represent characters and events in Anasazi myths." He turned to his father. "But isn't it illegal to dig up pottery like this and keep it or send it to friends?"

Fenton nodded. "It's illegal on public land, but Sam does most of his pottery-hunting on private ranch land, and keeping those pieces is legal. The question is," he added with a puzzled frown, "why he sent me such a valuable find at all. I haven't seen Sam in seven years."

"Does he explain in the letter?" Frank asked.

Fenton shook his head, studying the pages. "All this says is that he has something very important to tell me, and he wants us all to come out for a visit as soon as possible. He says while we're there we can help him explore an Anasazi

4

site he just found in a canyon near the Utah border.''

Before anyone could respond, Frank grabbed a photo as it fell from his father's letter and fluttered to the carpet.

"Wow! This is Tiffany?" he exclaimed.

"Let me see," Joe said, snatching the picture out of Frank's hand. It was of a white-haired man and a teenage girl leaning against a high rock wall covered with petroglyphs. The man had a white goatee and rimless spectacles. The girl had long, honey-colored hair, pale skin and hazel eyes, and a broad smile.

"*That's* Tiffany Gentle?" Joe said. "Hmm—maybe a visit to Arizona wouldn't be such a bad idea after all."

"Actually, it might be a *good* idea, Joe," Fenton said somberly. "The Kazakhstan government is still reeling after being liberated from the Soviet Union, and my trip there to help hook the country into the Interpol police network could take longer than a month."

Joe nodded. He knew that his father was eager to take on this important assignment in Kazakhstan.

"Plus Sam's letter worries me," Fenton admitted, "and I'd like you to check it out. His letters are usually full of jokes and family news, but this one is so stilted it's almost like reading code. If

5

Sam needs to talk about something 'important,' why doesn't he just pick up the phone?"

"Frank and I can fly out over Thanksgiving vacation and talk to Dr. Gentle. If there's a problem, we can call you in Kazakhstan."

"That sounds good," Fenton said slowly, "as long as your mother and your aunt don't mind."

"Certainly not," Gertrude Hardy responded. "Laura and I will do just fine on our own. We won't have to cook, and the peace and quiet will be good for a change."

"Then it's settled." Joe nudged his older brother. "Let's pack!"

Fenton smiled. "Whoa. You can wait till vacation starts. Meanwhile, I'll call Sam to tell him you're taking him up on his offer."

Several days later Joe and Frank were loading their suitcases into their aunt's car to go to the airport. Fenton Hardy had left for Kazakhstan the morning before.

"All set?" Gertrude Hardy asked, stepping onto the porch to check on them. "Oh dear," she added almost at once. "The phone."

"I'll get it," Frank said, running inside. Joe followed him into the kitchen. Their mother, Laura Hardy, was holding the receiver with a look of mild curiosity in her eyes.

"The operator says it's person to person from

Flagstaff," she said, handing Frank the receiver. "She won't say who's calling."

Frank took the receiver and put it to his ear. "This is Frank Hardy," he said. Immediately a man's harsh voice began speaking.

"Don't bother coming to Flagstaff. You're not wanted, understand?"

Stunned, Frank heard a click and then the dial tone.

"Who was that?" Joe asked as Frank stood staring quizzically at the receiver before slowly hanging it up.

"He didn't say," Frank said. "Whoever he was, he doesn't want us to take that flight."

"But Dad said Dr. Gentle couldn't wait for us to get there," Joe protested. "He said our visit was very important to him."

"This wasn't Dr. Gentle," Frank pointed out. "Maybe Dr. Gentle has an enemy who doesn't want us to know what's going on."

"Oh, no," Laura said. "Don't tell me you're being threatened already! Wouldn't it be better if you just stayed here?"

"We can't, Mom," Joe said. "Dr. Gentle is one of Dad's oldest friends. His letter made us suspect he's in some kind of trouble, and I think this phone call confirms it. We have to go."

Laura Hardy sighed. Frank sympathized with her. He knew she worried about them, but he also knew she wouldn't stop them. She was used to a husband who took on the most hazardous cases that came his way and two sons who seemed determined to follow in his footsteps.

"Be sure to get enough sleep," she said as she followed the boys out to Aunt Gertrude's car.

"We will, Mom," Joe said playfully as he and Frank climbed into the car. "We'll take our vitamins, too, and call you on Thanksgiving!"

Ten hours later Joe peered out the window of the airplane at the beautiful mountains of northern Arizona. The snow topping the steep, pine-covered peaks was washed pink by the setting sun.

"Did Dad say Dr. Gentle would meet us at the airport?" he asked Frank, who was reading a magazine in the seat beside him.

"Either Dr. Gentle or Tiffany," Frank answered. "By the way, Dr. Gentle told Dad he hoped you and I would be a good influence on Tiffany. He says that ever since her mother died a few years ago, Tiffany's been pretty rebellious."

"Could that be the important thing Dr. Gentle wanted to talk about?" Joe wondered out loud.

"I don't think so. You don't ask an old friend to fly out for a visit to talk about how to discipline your daughter."

Joe nodded, watching the mountains loom closer as the plane descended for its landing.

"What does Dr. Gentle do at the chemical plant?" he asked.

"Dad said he started out as an idealist in college. He dedicated himself to helping make sure everyone in the world has enough to eat. He took the job at Titan Chemical Industries to develop fertilizers and insecticides that would help farmers grow more crops. Now he's one of the top scientists at the plant." He shook his head. "It's hard to imagine a guy like that having any enemies."

Before Joe knew it, he and Frank had exited the plane and picked up their bags at the baggage claim area. When they stopped long enough to check, they realized that no one had come to meet them.

After half an hour of waiting, the boys went outside and hailed a taxi to take them to Dr. Gentle's house.

Dr. Gentle's home was located north of Flagstaff in a forest of long-needled pine trees on the steep side of a mountain. The taxi turned into the long drive, and Joe was startled as a dark green Jeep sped toward them. It swerved only at the last minute to avoid a crash with the taxi.

"I wonder if that could have been Dr. Gentle," Frank said, gazing through the rear window at the vehicle as the taxi driver shouted and waved his fist out the window.

"If it was, he was missing a parking light,"

9

Joe said. "And the left front fender was all bashed in."

The taxi driver calmed down and continued up the drive, which zigzagged through the towering pines as it climbed the mountain's slope. Finally the trees parted to reveal a sprawling modern house of stained redwood and fieldstone. The house had a magnificent view of the snow-covered San Francisco Peaks, north of Flagstaff. A battered blue Chevy was parked near the front door.

"The house looks dark," Frank observed as he and Joe unloaded their bags from the taxi. As the cab sped off they walked to the front door and pressed the bell.

"No one's home," Joe said after a minute.

"Try the door handle," Frank suggested. "Maybe there was an emergency, and Dr. Gentle left us a note inside."

Joe tried the handle. To his surprise, it turned. Gently Joe pushed the door open to reveal a spacious foyer.

Ahead of them the last rays of sunset flooded in through the enormous glass walls of the large living room. Joe stepped inside, followed by Frank.

"What a place," Joe murmured, but before he could say more he heard a loud click behind him.

"Put your hands in the air," a voice growled, "or I'll blow your heads off!"

Chapter
2

FRANK AND JOE slowly raised their arms. The lights snapped on, and a tall, dark-haired young man stepped from a hallway. He had a double-barreled shotgun leveled at the Hardys. Behind him stood a slender, honey-haired teenage girl in jeans and a pale blue sweater.

"Tiffany!" Frank said quickly. "It's me—Frank Hardy."

The man's aim wavered as the girl stepped forward. "Frank?" she said uncertainly. "I thought you weren't coming."

"Our dad couldn't make it, but we decided to make the trip without him," Joe said, putting his hands down as the young man lowered the shotgun. "I guess your dad forgot to tell you. Do you always answer the door armed?''

"The gun's not loaded," Tiffany said, glowering at Joe from beneath her thin eyelashes. She grabbed the shotgun from the young man, aimed it at the ceiling, and pulled the trigger. To Frank's relief, he heard only the loud *clack* of the hammer falling on an empty chamber.

Frank glanced at the tall, handsome young man who was watching him and Joe curiously. "I'm Frank Hardy," Frank said, extending a hand to the stranger. "This is my brother, Joe."

"Pleased to meet you," the young man said with a slight accent. "I'm Michael Slovik." He broke into a sheepish grin. "I'm sorry we scared you, but things have been a little weird here lately."

"Your dad was supposed to meet us at the airport, but he didn't show," Frank said to Tiffany.

Tiffany nodded. "Lesson number one," she said. "Never rely on Dad for anything—not when he's working. He left yesterday afternoon to hunt down petroglyphs in the canyons, I guess. He didn't leave me a note, so it's only a guess. He's been kind of mad at me lately and hasn't been telling me much about his activities. This guy is the main reason he's angry." She grinned over her shoulder at the lanky six-footer.

Slovik grinned back. "Her father resents me," Slovik said, "and he's been trying to interest Tiffany in other guys."

"Michael's a foreign exchange student at the university in Flagstaff," Tiffany said proudly. "I met him when he came to my high school to talk about the political situation in Eastern Europe. I'm going home with him next summer to meet his family."

Frank frowned. Dr. Gentle might be mad that Tiffany was dating a guy a few years older than she was, but that didn't seem a likely reason for him not to tell her where he was going and when he'd return. He wondered if the scientist's absence had anything to do with what he'd talked about in his letter. Frank knew this wasn't the time to ask.

"Is that his pottery collection?" Joe asked, peering into the living room. One entire wall was lined with glass-fronted display cases filled with antique pots of various shapes.

"That's only a small part of it," Tiffany said, leading them over to the cases. "The rest is on loan to a museum."

When Frank turned to study a pot, he caught Joe studying Tiffany and chuckled. Aunt Gertrude was right, he thought. If it wasn't for Joe's girlfriend, Vanessa—and for Michael Slovik— the blond-haired seventeen-year-old would be just Joe's type.

"Look, it's fine with me if you guys stay here," Tiffany was saying to Joe, "but I hope you don't expect me to baby-sit. I have plans with Michael tonight."

"We don't need a baby-sitter," Joe retorted a little angrily. "We'd just planned to get a bite to eat, talk to your father, and go to bed."

Tiffany exchanged a quick glance with Michael. He nodded once. "I'm sorry I've been rude," she said, "but I've been kind of worried and scared." She took a folded piece of paper from her pocket and handed it to Joe. "I found this at the front door a couple of minutes before you two showed up. That's why we didn't answer the door—we were scared that you'd left this note."

Joe unfolded the paper and read it out loud as Frank looked on. " 'Dr. Gentle: Stop your research now, or you'll pay for your crimes!' "

"What research?" Joe asked.

"At the chemical manufacturing company he works for," Tiffany said. "Some people think the scientists are designing pesticides to kill people instead of insects. And Dad thinks one of those people must be sending him notes."

"How many have turned up?" Frank asked.

"This is the fifth that I know of," Tiffany told him. "But Dad could have gotten more and just not told me."

14

"Do you really think your dad's out scouting petroglyphs?" Frank asked.

"Why?" Tiffany said. "Do you think something's happened to him? I can't believe the people who wrote these notes would actually do anything to harm him. He spends hours in the mountains, and that's where I have to believe he is." Her tone turned resentful. "Ever since my mom died, a few years ago, the only thing that makes him happy is to hang out in the mountains. The only time I have his full attention is when he's telling me to stay away from Michael."

"You said you found this note just before we got here," Joe said, interrupting. "A green Jeep with a smashed front fender almost knocked us off the road as we turned into your drive. Do you know anyone with a Jeep like that? The driver probably left the note."

Tiffany explained to Michael, "My dad said Frank and Joe are ace detectives." Turning back to Joe, she said, "No, I can't think of anyone with a Jeep like that. Sorry."

"We've got to get going," Michael said, checking his watch. "The movie starts at half past eight."

"I'm ready." Tiffany started back to the entryway, where she grabbed her purse from a table near the front door. "You guys can stay in the guest room. It's down the hall and faces the pool," she said, opening the door. "Help your-selves to food and stuff. If Dad shows up, tell him I'll be back by midnight—if he cares."

"There's something very weird going on here, Joe, and these notes may be the key," Frank said after the door closed behind the couple. He peered out the window to see Michael's dusty Chevy pulling away.

"And the green Jeep obviously plays a part in this, too," Joe agreed. "But I'm beat. All I want to find are the kitchen and our room. Maybe Tiffany's right—by the time we've eaten, Dr. Gentle will be back with dust on his boots."

"Or maybe," Frank murmured, "we have a very serious mystery on our hands."

Bright morning light nearly blinded Frank as he opened his eyes. The Hardys' room was at the far end of the Gentles' rambling house, with sliding glass doors leading straight out to the pool. The intense light wasn't half as painful as the rock music blasting at top volume over the patio speakers.

"Sounds like Tiffany's up," Frank heard his brother moan from the other twin bed.

"Yeah, and it's a safe bet that her dad's not home. Come on—let's go get breakfast."

Fifteen minutes later, having showered and dressed, the Hardys joined Tiffany at the break-fast table on the patio. "I hope you like scrambled eggs," she shouted over the music, helping herself to a huge scoop along with several strips of bacon.

"There's no way I can like anything with music that loud," Frank grumbled, pouring himself orange juice.

Frank found the stereo and turned the volume down. Then he returned to the table, where Tiffany and Joe were wolfing down their food. "It looks like your father didn't come home," Frank said to Tiffany.

"So what else is new?" Tiffany shrugged but couldn't hide the hurt expression that flitted across her face. "He probably went straight from his campsite to his office. He usually does that when he gets really engrossed in a new find."

"Doesn't he worry about leaving you alone?" Joe asked, reaching for another piece of bacon.

"I'm used to taking care of myself," Tiffany said defensively. "And to tell you the truth, it's fine with me. When Dad's gone I get to spend time with Michael. And now I have a week's vacation, so I have lots of time for Michael."

After breakfast Tiffany gave the boys the keys to the Gentles' red half-ton pickup and directions to Titan Chemical Industries on the outskirts of Flagstaff. On the way down the mountain Joe rolled down his window and deeply breathed in the cool mountain air. "This is what I call a great drive to work," he said, gazing through the windshield at the surrounding mountains.

"The first part of the drive was nice," Frank said, pulling onto a narrow road that led to the industrial park housing Titan Chemicals. "But the final few hundred feet look pretty scary."

Joe's eyes widened as he took in the scene in front of him. "I see what you mean," he said. The chemical company was a sprawling complex of buildings surrounded by a high chain-link fence topped with barbed wire. A huge sign above the front gate read, TCI—Pesticides, Herbicides, Agricultural Products. Just outside the fence were a couple of vans with satellite dishes on their roofs and radio and television call letters painted on their sides. Several dozen people lined both sides of the road, waving signs and chanting.

"It's a demonstration," Joe said. He peered at the signs. " 'No more chemical war!' " he read aloud. " 'Ban chemical weapons!' "

"It looks more like a mob than a demonstration," Frank said as he maneuvered the truck between the rows of demonstrators.

Frank idled past the crowd and a few police officers before stopping the truck in front of the guardhouse. Frank noticed a look of surprise cross the gray-haired security guard's face when he saw the truck.

"We're here to see Dr. Sam Gentle," Frank said, shouting over the noise of the chanting.

"This is his truck, ain't it?" demanded the guard.

Frank nodded. "We're guests of his—Frank and Joe Hardy. His daughter said we could find him here."

"He's not in yet. Matter of fact, the company president asked me to keep a lookout for him." He pointed to a glass office building several hundred feet away. A helicopter bearing the TCI logo was parked on a landing pad on the roof. "I think Dr. Sholdice said he might want to talk to you. I'll call ahead and ask."

"Sounds mysterious," Joe remarked as Frank was cleared and drove through the gate to park in front of the office building. "I wonder why the president wants to see us."

"Only one way to find out," Frank replied, and he led the way through the front doors.

Moments later the Hardys entered Titan Chemical Industries' executive offices on the second floor and were quickly escorted through a pair of heavy wooden doors into the president's huge office. Inside, a tall, thin man dressed casually in shirt sleeves and a bolo tie sat behind a huge mahogany desk, signing a stack of official-looking papers.

"I'm Dr. Armand Sholdice. Please have a seat," he said after Frank and Joe had introduced themselves. "I remember hearing about you from Sam. You're detectives, aren't you—the sons of the famous Fenton Hardy?"

"That's right," Frank said as he and Joe sat in a pair of matching leather chairs facing Sholdice. "This is an impressive company you have here—especially the helicopter on your roof."

Sholdice smiled. "Yes, I was a helicopter pilot in the army many years ago. I keep flying as a hobby. It's very handy when I want to avoid demonstrators at my front gate. I just go over them." He laughed.

"Who are those people?" Joe asked, his attention wandering out the window to the demonstrators. Several of them seemed to be arguing with a couple of police officers. They waved their signs to emphasize their points.

"Extremists," Sholdice said with a single dismissive wave. "The trouble started with Garth Hudson, a fellow who used to work here. When we fired him he organized a group to harass us. The group calls itself the AWA—for Anti-War Alliance—but in reality they're misguided fools."

"Why did you fire Hudson?" Frank asked.

"Personality problems. But forget about him," Dr. Sholdice said abruptly. "Listen, I'm hoping you boys can tell me where Sam is. He isn't here and didn't even call in today.''

"That's why *we* came *here,*" Joe told him worriedly. "When we arrived yesterday, his daughter said she hadn't seen him since the day before yesterday.''

"That's bad," Sholdice said with a grim expression. "You see"—Sholdice gazed directly at the two boys—"a warrant has been issued for Dr. Gentle's arrest.''

Frank and Joe were astonished.

"Sometime yesterday he stole some computer disks containing the files on a new and secret formula for a weed killer—an herbicide he created that will revolutionize agriculture,'' Sholdice continued. "The company's competitors would love to get their hands on the formula before it's patented, and I think Gentle's out to sell it to the highest bidder.''

"Why do you think Dr. Gentle stole them?" Frank asked.

"It could only have been him," said Sholdice. "He was the senior scientist on the project, and the disks containing the formula were kept in a safe in his office. Several people saw him leave work at lunchtime the day before yesterday, carrying his briefcase. The disks were reported missing right after that, and he and the disks haven't been seen since.''

"Dr. Sholdice, I'm sure Sam Gentle didn't

steal those tapes," Joe said hotly. "Why would a thief invite a couple of detectives out here if he was planning to steal something?"

"Maybe he decided to take them after he'd invited you," the president said with a shrug. "He's been acting strange lately. Who knows what was on his mind?"

Sholdice leaned back in his chair. "Perhaps you or your father could help the good doctor, since he's an old family friend."

"What do you mean?" Joe asked suspiciously.

Sholdice sighed. "This formula is terribly important to us," he answered carefully. "I would consider dropping charges against Dr. Gentle, no questions asked, if the disks were returned."

Abruptly Dr. Sholdice stood and quickly escorted the boys out.

The security guard waved the Hardys through the gate, and Frank drove slowly off the factory grounds. The protestors outside seemed to go wild. "Do you think they recognize this truck?" Frank asked.

"They must," Joe responded, watching amazed as one demonstrator hit the hood of the truck with a crudely painted sign. Several officers arrived to push the demonstrators back behind a wooden barricade, but Joe could still see their angry faces as the truck moved slowly past.

"Look at that guy," Frank said, pointing out a lanky, bearded protestor.

"Let's just get out of here," Joe muttered tensely.

"I'm trying," Frank said. He had to brake sharply as the bearded demonstrator threw himself in front of the truck. A young woman with a long brown ponytail pulled him back just before the truck would have hit him. Frank and Joe watched as several of the police officers grabbed the pair and pushed them back behind the barricades.

"Dr. Gentle will get what he deserves!" the man screamed over the officer's shoulder at the Hardys. "That murderer deserves to die!"

Chapter

3

"Now!" Joe said as all the other protestors were hustled out of the way.

Frank pressed down on the accelerator. The truck moved past the chanting, angry crowd toward the main road. "Could that have been Garth Hudson, the guy who was fired?" Frank asked.

"Probably," Joe said. "Nobody else seemed that wound up. Now I see what Dr. Sholdice meant by 'personality problems.' Dr. Gentle probably took a day off just to get away from that mob."

Frank steered the truck off the highway, glancing at his brother. "You don't really think Dr. Gentle stole those files, do you?" he asked.

"Of course not," Joe said. Then his expression faltered. "At least not without a good reason. Dad's always told us what a great humanitarian Sam Gentle is—you know that."

"I know," Frank said with a sigh, and he headed for Gentle's house. "I just wish I knew where he is."

As the truck rounded the last curve up the long drive to the house, Frank could see Michael Slovik's battered Chevy parked in front. Leading the way inside, Frank found Michael and Tiffany on the living room sofa, watching a tennis match on TV.

"Did you find Dad?" Tiffany asked as the Hardys joined them.

"Nope," Frank answered cautiously. "He wasn't at the plant."

"I did figure out that he's got to be camping," Tiffany said. "After you left I checked the attic for his camping equipment. It's not there. He must have lost track of time and forgotten to go into work."

"Where would he have gone exactly?" Joe asked.

"Wolf's Tooth Canyon is my guess," Tiffany told him. "It's his latest find—about ten feet wide, sixty feet deep, and jam-packed with petroglyphs. The canyon's about a three-hour drive away."

Frank bit his lip, wondering how to tell Tiffany about the warrant for her father's arrest. He decided to be straightforward. "We found out a few things, too," he told her. "Your dad's boss, Dr. Sholdice, told us that some very valuable computer disks were stolen from TCI. I hate to have to tell you this, but Sholdice thinks your father stole them. There's a warrant out for his arrest."

"Dad?" Tiffany stared at Frank in shock as Michael scooted closer and put an arm around her.

"Why would he do this?" Michael demanded.

"That's the million-dollar question," Joe told him. "You haven't seen any unidentified computer disks here at the house?"

Tiffany looked stunned. Then she lifted her chin. "I wouldn't know what disks are here," she said. "But I do know one thing. There's no way my dad took those disks. He's dedicated his whole life to that company."

"Then let's go find him," Joe said, moving toward the door. "I'll drive."

"No." Tiffany drew back tighter against Michael's arm. "You go without me. I'll show you the route to the canyon on a map. If Dad wants to talk to me, he knows where I am."

"Tiffany, you're as stubborn as you were when you were little," Joe said impatiently as he and Frank moved to the door. "Your father's in trouble. He needs your help."

Tiffany's eyes and lips narrowed to slits. "I'm not going," she said. "But if you find Dad, tell him—well, give him my best."

" 'Give him my best'?" Joe repeated a few minutes later as the two Hardys climbed back into the red truck and sped down the drive. "There's a warrant out for her father's arrest, and that's all she has to say?"

"They're having a fight," Frank said, studying the map she had given them. "Dr. Gentle's been preoccupied, I guess, and Tiffany's fed up with being left alone."

"That must be what she sees in Michael," Joe grumbled, shifting gears. "He does pay attention to her, that's for sure."

Frank chuckled. Joe didn't seem to realize that Michael's looks and intelligence might have something to do with Tiffany's attraction to him. "There's no time to stop for lunch," he said. "How about picking up something and eating in the truck?"

The Hardys headed toward the Grand Canyon and the Utah border. According to Tiffany's map, the Colorado River was a hundred miles ahead. On the other side of it the Hardys would turn west and drive another forty miles to Wolf's Tooth Canyon.

"This is more like it," Joe said through a

mouthful of taco as Flagstaff's pine forests began to fade away. The green slopes were replaced by the rolling treeless hills, red sand, and sagebrush of the Painted Desert.

After stopping to buy soda at a trading post in Marble Canyon, the Hardys crossed a bridge over the Grand Canyon to the northern side of the Colorado River. "Wow," Joe said, looking down at the striped colors of the immense cliff walls, "the Grand Canyon must be the only place in the world that looks bigger when you visit it again."

"It is getting bigger," Frank pointed out. "The river's still wearing away the rock—though I seriously doubt you can tell the difference from the way it was seven years ago. Your turn to drive," he added, pulling the truck over to the side of the road. "I'm tired of missing all the scenery."

Soon after Joe took the wheel, he turned the truck onto a narrow two-lane road that led across the rolling hills. When the brothers reached the crest of a hill overlooking a wide, arid canyon, they saw the blacktop road wind down the steep sides of the canyon like a curl of licorice. At the bottom it crossed a thin, white line that marked the gravel bed of a narrow, dried-up river, then curved lazily back up the far wall of the canyon.

"I'm getting thirsty just looking at this dry

land," Joe remarked. "And I've already finished my soda. You'll have to let me have some of yours if I'm going to drive."

Frank shook his head and passed his can to Joe. Then Joe shifted down into second gear and maneuvered slowly around the hairpin turns that led down into the canyon. They crossed the riverbed and then went up again. Signs warned of rock falls on one side, and on the other a sheer drop of hundreds of feet meant certain death if Joe missed a turn. Finally, after nearly forty-five minutes, the truck took the final curve and surfaced on a plateau. Ahead Joe could see the soft, undulating peaks of a low mountain range.

"The turnoff should be about half a mile from here," Frank said, studying the map Tiffany had drawn for them. "We take that road for two miles to the edge of another valley with sides gentle enough to hike down. Wolf's Tooth Canyon is at the bottom of the valley. From what Tiffany said, we can't miss it. It's a narrow ten-foot chasm cut sixty feet into the valley floor."

It wasn't long before Joe spotted a sign with yellow letters spelling Wolf's Tooth Canyon and an arrow pointing to the west. "I'm glad Tiffany suggested we load camping equipment into the back of the truck," Joe remarked as he turned onto the rough gravel road. "We can stay overnight if we have to."

"It shouldn't be hard to spot Dr. Gentle's Land Rover out here—if he is here," Frank remarked.

"There's the canyon," Frank added a few minutes later, pointing down into the valley. Joe saw a thin, dark crevasse snaking along the bottom. It was as if the boulder-strewn valley had been split in two.

"It looks like it leads to the center of the earth," Joe remarked.

"You're right—I can't see the bottom," Frank replied. "But Tiffany said there's a riverbed down there."

"There's the head of the trail," Joe said, pointing ahead to a small brown sign. "And look— there's a Land Rover!"

Before Frank could focus on the Rover, another vehicle swung around a sharp turn and headed straight for the Hardys.

"Hey!" Joe shouted, steering hard to the right until the pickup nearly ran off the road. As the vehicle passed, Joe caught a glimpse of a crumpled left front fender and missing parking light. "That's the green Jeep we saw at the Gentles' house last night!" he shouted, pulling back onto the road.

"Turn around!" Frank ordered excitedly. "Follow it!"

The road was too narrow to make a U-turn, and any mistake could mean driving off the edge into the canyon. Joe rammed the gearshift into reverse and backed up, jolting both Hardys in their seats. Frank turned around and tried to make out the license number of the speeding Jeep through the rear window, but the plate was obscured by dust thrown up from the Jeep.

By the time Joe had enough space to turn the pickup, the Jeep was fading behind a thick cloud of fine gravel far up the road. Joe gunned the pickup. Letting the shocks carry the bone-jouncing strain of ruts and rocks, he covered the two miles of road in scant minutes. By the time he reached the road on the top of the plateau, the Jeep had disappeared.

"It's fifty-fifty which way he went," Joe said, looking right and left along the empty road. "You call it."

"Go right," Frank instructed. "The driver's probably heading back to Flagstaff."

Joe gunned the engine and turned onto the road. A few moments later they reached the rim of the wide canyon.

"There it is!" Frank cried excitedly. The Jeep was visible far below them, negotiating the last sharp turns before reaching the valley floor.

"Here goes nothing," Joe said grimly, tightening his hands on the steering wheel. He pushed down on the gas pedal and took the first hairpin curve into the valley as fast as he dared, then accelerated into the next straight stretch.

"Faster!" Frank said, keeping his eyes on the Jeep.

"I'm trying!" Joe retorted. As the narrow road became steeper the half-ton pickup gathered momentum. Joe was forced to brake almost constantly to slow their descent.

"He's crossed the river already," Frank reported.

"I hear you," Joe muttered, quickly studying the sharp turn ahead where the road swung to the left around the side of a cliff. On their right was another precipitous drop.

Joe braked sharply, then turned tightly to the left. Suddenly the road seemed to disappear under the front wheels.

"Watch out!" Frank shouted.

Joe frantically turned the steering wheel farther to the left, but he was too late. The back wheels spun without holding on the loose gravel road as the end fishtailed crazily. Before Joe could gain control of the truck, the passenger side of the cab swung farther to the right. Next Joe felt the cab dropping into empty space!

Chapter

4

JOE SMASHED the brake and clutch to the floor and slammed the gearshift into reverse. He let go of the brake and popped the clutch. The smell of burned rubber filled the air as the pickup backed up a few inches, then lurched to a halt, bouncing on its own suspension.

"You want to get out?" Frank asked stiffly.

"Do you think I should?" From where Joe sat it looked as though both front wheels were over the edge of the cliff. Beyond the windshield was only vast blue sky, the lowering sun, and the tiny green Jeep quickly climbing the opposite side of the valley. "The smallest movement could send us over the edge," Joe pointed out.

"We have to get out of here," Frank said.

"There's nothing but air outside my door. What about yours?"

Hardly daring to breathe, Joe leaned inches to the left to look out his open window. To his surprise, he saw road beneath the truck. Gaining courage, Joe stuck his head out farther. It looked as though a giant had bitten a chunk out of the side of the road, and the truck's left front wheel was barely resting on the broken edge.

"Okay," Joe said. "It's up to me to move first." Taking a deep breath, he slowly opened his door. With each movement a part of him waited for the truck to tip forward and plunge into the valley below. He edged himself along the seat and slowly lowered himself to the road.

"Boy, the ground feels good," he said aloud. Then he remembered his brother. Stepping back, he could see that although the rear wheels were firmly planted on the road, the front wheel on Frank's side was hanging in space.

"Slide out slowly on my side, Frank," he called to his brother. "You'll be okay."

Joe watched as Frank edged himself past the steering wheel. The truck rocked slightly, then settled again. Joe stepped forward to grab his brother's hand as Frank reached for solid ground with one foot.

Suddenly the truck jerked forward. Frank threw himself out of the truck, knocking Joe over as he landed on the road. For a moment the brothers froze, waiting to hear the truck crash on the rocks below.

No sound came. The truck was still hanging over the edge, its front end seesawing crazily.

"That was close," Frank said, climbing to his feet. "Where's the Jeep?"

"There," Joe said, standing and pointing at a green speck zigzagging up the opposite wall of the valley. The Jeep had almost finished its climb.

"Did you get a look at the driver when it passed us?" Frank asked.

Joe shook his head. "The windows were tinted. I couldn't see inside."

"I bet it's not the last time we see it, anyway," Frank predicted, brushing dust off his jeans.

"That all depends on whether we get out of here." Joe glanced at the useless truck. "This isn't exactly a well-traveled road, and I haven't seen a gas station for miles."

"There's a winch in the back," Frank told him, moving to the rear of the truck. "Tiffany showed it to me when she helped us load the camping gear. She said it's standard equipment on trucks in the Southwest because of the rough roads."

"Great!" Joe spotted a large boulder leaning against the limestone cliff across the road. "We can string the cable around that rock and pull the truck back on the road."

Frank found the winch in a metal box welded to the back of the pickup. The winch looked like a giant metal fishing reel with steel cable wrapped around it and an iron hook at the end of the cable. As Frank attached the winch to the rear bumper of the pickup, Joe walked toward the boulder, unwinding the cable as he went.

After coiling the cable around the boulder, Joe secured the hook to the cable. "When I came to Arizona I never thought I'd be lassoing rocks," he remarked as Frank began turning the handle on the winch. Frank grinned as the cable tightened, and slowly the half-ton pickup began to move. Moments later the front wheels were pulled back onto the road.

"All right!" Joe said, slapping his brother a high-five when the truck was firmly on solid ground. "What now?" he asked as he checked the sky, which was streaked with pink and purple rays from the setting sun.

"That Land Rover back by the trailhead," Frank said, "has to be Dr. Gentle's. Let's go back and see if we can find him before it gets dark."

"Good idea." Joe climbed into the passenger seat, casting a quick look at the sun. "We only have about an hour and a half of light."

After loading the winch into the toolbox, Frank drove the truck back to where the dusty Land Rover was parked. He stopped the truck and got out, then peered through the Rover's windows at coiled ropes, climbing equipment, a well-worn pair of hiking boots, and half a dozen plastic bottles of drinking water. "He sure was prepared," Frank remarked as Joe wandered toward the small sign that read Trailhead.

"There's the trail that runs down into the valley," Joe said, peering over the ledge. Frank joined him and saw the path meandering among scrub oak trees whose twisted roots clung to the canyon's stone walls. Massive limestone boulders had broken away from the walls and were strewn randomly along the path.

"Let's get our packs and go," Frank said, heading back toward the truck. "We don't have much daylight left."

The brothers slipped on their backpacks and canteens before they began the hike down. It was an easygoing hike, with the trail clearly marked. On sections where the ground leveled off they even walked through tall grass and between oaks. When it turned steep again, the ground turned stony, and the trees were replaced by an occasional yucca plant and a few short, twisted mesquite trees.

"There it is! The slot canyon!" Joe said, hurrying ahead as they reached a plateau of solid limestone at the bottom of the valley. Fifty feet away a dark gap was visible in the rock. The last rays of sunlight slid partway down one side of the opening, illuminating horizontal lines of different colors in the face of the rock. Each layer, Frank realized, represented thousands of years of geological history, and there were hundreds of layers.

"It must have taken millions of years for a stream to cut this out," Joe said, echoing his brother's thoughts as he stood on the edge of the crevasse and looked down to the bottom. The shifting light penetrated only partly into the deep crack, casting a spectrum of light and shadow that moved slowly across the rock walls like waves.

Joe picked up a pebble and tossed it over the edge. Seconds ticked past. Finally they heard a distant thunk far below, and then its echo repeating itself up and down the gap.

"Ready to explore?" Frank asked, leading the way along the rim of the slot canyon.

"You bet." Joe's voice betrayed his excitement. He followed Frank several hundred feet to a place where the crevasse widened to almost thirty feet. The ground on one side had crumbled away, spilling down into the canyon. Frank spotted a thin path strewn with broken rock that wove down among the immense slabs of limestone.

Carefully Frank picked his way down into the narrow canyon, followed closely by Joe. The sheer walls towered higher and higher overhead, and Frank noticed that the air quickly turned cool. By the time they were halfway down, they had left the last shafts of sunlight behind and entered permanent shadow.

"This is where the Anasazi lived?" Joe asked, his voice echoing against the walls behind Frank.

"Not this far down, I bet," Frank replied, leading the way to the narrow bottom of the canyon. "It probably never gets completely light in here. And look—the bottom's only six feet wide."

As they reached the canyon floor, Frank switched on his flashlight and saw a thin line of fine, light gravel running down the center. It was slightly muddy with remnants of the last rain.

"That must be Wolf's Tooth Creek, or what's left of it at this time of year," Frank said.

Joe was peering closely at the gravel floor. "Look, Frank," he said. "Footprints." He knelt to examine them closely in the harsh beam from his flashlight. Frank moved closer. The large prints showed distinctive heel marks with a thick herringbone thread. The edges of the print were just beginning to dry.

"It looks like these were made by hiking boots within the last few hours," Joe said. "They seem to be coming from up there."

Frank looked behind him, where Joe was

39

pointing. "Someone must have climbed down here on another trail," he said.

Joe pointed to a spot a short distance ahead. "Look. There's a different set of prints up there."

Shining his light on the second set of prints, Frank saw that these were larger but just as fresh.

"It looks like this person entered the canyon and left again," he said, studying the tracks. "The same prints go back the other way, overlapping the first ones."

"Do you think one of these people was Dr. Gentle?" Joe asked.

"It makes sense, but let's find out," Frank replied, shining his light down the riverbed.

The brothers followed the two sets of prints along the floor of the canyon. They had walked about fifty feet when they saw a long, dark object lying across the canyon floor ahead of them.

Frank aimed his flashlight at the object. As they approached it Frank made out first a snow-white beard, then the face.

"Dr. Gentle!" he said, racing forward, Joe right behind him.

They were too late. The bruised and bloodied body lay motionless on the ground. Dr. Gentle's dead eyes gazed vacantly at the thin crack of sky high above the canyon.

Chapter

5

FRANK LIFTED the man's arm. The skin was cold. His fingers groped along the wrist, feeling for a pulse. There was none. "The body's not stiff yet," he said. "He must have died within the last couple of hours."

"I can't believe it," Joe said quietly. The scientist's face and arms were covered with scratches, and there was an ugly wound on his forehead. He had fallen on his back, partly covering a large nylon backpack that had split its seams. Around him were scattered the contents of the backpack: plastic bags of trail mix, a groundsheet, and the ripped remains of a sleeping bag.

"Frank, check this out," Joe said.

Joe knelt at Dr. Gentle's feet and examined the soles of his hiking boots. "These boots made the tracks with the herringbone pattern. But we found those tracks past the body. How did he get back here?"

Frank shone his light up the walls of the towering canyon. More camping equipment was strewn along outcroppings of rock. An aluminum pan dangled from a narrow ledge. White down from the sleeping bag was scattered over the rocks. "He must have climbed to the top and then fallen," Frank said grimly.

Joe frowned. "The other set of prints lead to the body, stop, and then head back to the trail again," he said. "It's as if somebody knew the body was here and came down to check it out."

"Maybe they belong to the driver of the green Jeep we saw," Frank suggested. "He sure was eager to get away."

"You think someone pushed Dr. Gentle into the canyon?" Joe asked, alarmed.

"It seems that way to me. We'll have to climb back up to the top and check it out," Frank replied. He played the flashlight's beam over the camping equipment scattered around the body. "I don't see any computer disks," he pointed out. "Dr. Sholdice must have been wrong—unless the person who pushed Dr. Gentle found the disks."

The Hardys quickly retraced their steps to the

top of the slot canyon. "This must be about where he fell from," Frank said to Joe as they stood at the top of the crevasse, looking down. "He was probably hiking back to his car."

"There's no sign of a struggle," Joe commented, studying the rocky ground. "But it would be almost impossible to find anything on a hard surface like this. Come on—we'd better call the police."

After following the trail up out of the valley, Frank and Joe examined the area around the Land Rover, but there were too many tire tracks to make any sense out of them. Finally they climbed into the pickup truck and drove away from the canyon.

"I keep thinking about that letter Dr. Gentle wrote to Dad," Frank said, breaking the silence. "He wrote that he had something important to tell Dad."

Joe nodded and remembered the threatening letters Tiffany had described him getting.

"No time to think about it now, I guess," Frank said, pointing to a ranch house to the right of the road. "Let's ask to call the police from there. I think we have to tell Tiffany in person."

Less than an hour later Frank and Joe were leading a squad of search-and-rescue volunteers, several paramedics, a sheriff, and a pair of state troopers back to the top of the slot canyon.

Night had fallen, and the jet black sky was riveted with silver stars. The state troopers set up portable lights while the paramedics and rescue crew descended to bring the body out.

Frank and Joe waited with the sheriff, a short, potbellied man named Wilkins from the nearby town of Page. He worked with an efficient, calm manner.

"We found an arrest warrant for Sam Gentle in our computers," he told Frank and Joe.

"Nothing's been proven," Frank pointed out.

Joe saw lights moving toward them in the sky. The distant *thwip* of a helicopter quickly grew louder. When it came into view Joe immediately saw the TCI logo on the fuselage. The chopper hovered for a moment, then touched down fifty feet away. To Joe's surprise, Dr. Sholdice stepped out.

"I got a call from the Flagstaff state troopers about this," Sholdice said sadly, introducing himself to the sheriff. He turned to Frank and Joe. "Terrible tragedy. He was a brilliant scientist. Was there any sign of the formula he stole when you found the body?"

Frank stiffened. "If you mean the missing computer disks, we didn't find them," he said.

"But we saw a green Jeep leaving here," Joe added. The Hardys told Sheriff Wilkins about the mystery vehicle they had seen twice, and also about the threatening letters Dr. Gentle had received. They then described the confusing trail of footprints below.

"Dr. Gentle showed me those letters," Sholdice said dismissively. "Obviously they were written by one of the antiwar demonstrators camped outside our plant—probably Garth Hudson, the man we fired."

"What about the Jeep?" Frank asked. "Do you know anyone who owns one like that?"

Sholdice shrugged. "No, I don't. But I'll bet your Jeep driver never got those disks. I bet Gentle hid them somewhere in the canyon."

Joe was taken aback. "Why?"

"So whoever was in the green Jeep wouldn't find them, I assume," Sholdice said.

Frank frowned. Joe knew he was wondering whether Sholdice's theory could be true. Could Sam Gentle have stolen the formula after all?

"It seems to me that Dr. Gentle would be more likely to hide computer data in his office than out here," Joe said. "Frank and I should take a look around that office. Maybe we can find some kind of clue there."

"It's already been thoroughly searched by the police," Sholdice told them with a sigh. "But you're welcome to check—tonight, if you want."

Sholdice left in his helicopter a short time later. Frank and Joe waited until Dr. Gentle's body was lifted up from the canyon. By then it was almost nine o'clock.

"Let's take Dr. Sholdice up on his offer and check out Sam Gentle's office tonight," Frank suggested.

"It'll be midnight before we get back there," Joe said, "but that's fine with me, as long as we get a bite to eat on the road. The state troopers will tell Tiffany, and then we can be with her later. Actually, she'll probably want to be with Michael."

Three hours and three burgers later the brothers arrived at the gates of TCI. It was just after midnight, but the security guard was expecting them—and Sholdice was waiting in his office, hunched over a pile of papers on his desk.

Sholdice led Frank and Joe to a long, hangar-like building covered with blue aluminum siding and a metal roof. Dr. Gentle's office was one of many along a brightly lit central corridor.

"This is it," the company president said as he turned the lights on. "I'm afraid Dr. Gentle wasn't concerned about being tidy."

Frank scanned the room. Books and papers covered with scrawled equations were stacked on every available flat surface. Behind the desk a large iron safe stood open. Its shelves were bare.

"That's where the disks were kept," Sholdice explained.

Frank noticed half a dozen black hardcover notebooks piled on a credenza behind Dr. Gentle's desk and picked one up. Page after page was covered with spidery handwriting and precise reproductions of the stick figures and symbols of ancient petroglyphs.

"These must be the notes Dr. Gentle kept on his archaeological outings," Frank said, turning the pages. He saw that the scientist had carefully drawn maps of various canyons, marking different points where the petroglyphs had been found.

"Let's take them back to the house to study," Joe suggested. "Maybe we'll find a clue as to what happened to Dr. Gentle in these notes."

Dr. Sholdice seemed reluctant. "With Dr. Gentle dead, I feel responsible—"

"They won't go any farther than Sam Gentle's house," Joe assured him. "I guess they belong to his daughter now, anyway."

Arriving back at the Gentles' at a little before two in the morning, the Hardys were surprised to find Tiffany watching television and drinking a soda. A roaring fire in the massive stone fireplace warmed the room.

When she saw Frank and Joe, Tiffany smiled. Frank knew then that the police hadn't con-

tacted her. Maybe it was a bureaucratic foul-up.
Maybe they had assumed Frank and Joe would
inform her of her father's death.

"I was wondering if you guys had abandoned
ship," Tiffany said. "Dad's still not back."

Frank shuffled nervously, unable to return her
smile. "Tiffany, I take it the police haven't been
here or called you tonight?"

"No." Tiffany's smile began to fade. "Why?"

"Well—there's been an accident," Frank said
softly. "I'm sorry—it's your father."

"He was at Wolf's Tooth Canyon," Joe
added. "We think he fell—"

Tiffany went pale. "From where? Is he—"

Frank sat down next to her on the sofa. "I'm
sorry, Tiffany. We think he fell from the rim."
He took her hands in his.

"Oh, no," Tiffany whispered. Tears filled her
eyes. "I don't believe this."

"Can I get you anything?" Joe asked.

Tiffany shook her head miserably. "This is my
fault," she said. "Dad and I had that terrible
argument before he left the day before yesterday. He said Michael was too old for me, and
he didn't want me to see him anymore. Dad
made me so mad that I told him I never wanted
to see *him* again." Tears were running down her
face now.

"I—I told myself I didn't care if he never
came back!" she stammered.

"You didn't mean it, and he knew it," Joe said. "All kids say mean things to their parents sometimes."

"Your dad cared about you," Frank said softly. "And he knew you cared about him."

Tiffany flushed as if overcome by shame. She turned her head away. "I have a confession to make," she said in a whisper. "I didn't want you to come here. Dad hoped you'd distract me from Michael, but I didn't want to be distracted. I made Michael call your house in Bayport and tell you not to come."

"Michael was our anonymous caller?" Frank said.

Tiffany nodded miserably.

"Obviously it didn't work," she said.

"Tiffany, your father said he had something important to tell us. Our dad was really worried about him. And there are all those threatening notes you told us about. Was he in some kind of trouble? You don't have to talk about it now, but you might want to think about it."

Tiffany looked at Frank curiously. "Actually, it will do me good to talk a bit. If Dad was in trouble, he never mentioned it to me," she said. "Of course, there were the demonstrators who were against him—especially Garth Hudson, who used to work for him. Do you think this could have anything to do with that missing formula?"

The brothers shrugged. "We don't know for sure."

Frank cleared his throat and took her hand again. "We may be wrong, but it's possible your father was pushed from the cliff."

Tiffany turned pale. "He was murdered?"

"It's possible." Joe squeezed Tiffany's shoulder. "But I promise we won't stop asking questions until we know for sure."

The boys stayed up late talking with Tiffany, or rather letting her talk until she was tired enough to sleep.

The next morning Joe woke at nine, dressed quickly, and headed for the kitchen. There he found Frank sitting with a glass of orange juice and Dr. Gentle's notebooks.

"Each expedition he went on is dated," Frank said. "The most recent date is from three months ago, so his last book seems to be missing."

Joe poured himself a glass of juice. "You're right. He obviously made detailed notes every time he went to the canyons, so he must have had a notebook with him."

"I don't remember seeing one in the canyon," Frank pointed out.

Joe nodded slowly. "I guess we could drive back up there and look around."

"Before we do I want to talk to Garth Hudson, the leader of the Anti-War Alliance," Frank said.

Joe sat down at the table and flipped through Gentle's notebook while Frank tried to locate Hudson and his alliance. A few minutes later Frank hung up the phone. "No one was in," he told his brother. "But the answering machine says the Anti-War Alliance's office is in a town called New Berlin. I've never heard of it. Have you?"

"I have," said Tiffany, who had entered the kitchen just as Frank finished speaking. Joe noticed that her eyes were swollen as if she had been crying all night.

"New Berlin is a ghost town near an abandoned silver mine on Slate Mountain," she told the boys as she sat at the table. "The silver ran out almost a hundred years ago. Now a bunch of artists, jewelry designers, and New Age types live there. Why?"

"We thought we'd take a drive out that way," Frank said evasively. "Unless you'd like us to stay here and help you."

Tiffany ran a hand through her honey-colored hair. "Thanks for the offer, but I'm going to call my aunt in Phoenix," she said. "She's my closest relative, and she'll help me call people and deal with the—the arrangements," she finished with a defeated look on her face.

"You're sure there isn't anything we can do to help?" Joe asked softly.

"There is one thing." Tiffany looked at him with a determined expression. "Find out what happened to my dad in that canyon," she said.

After breakfast Frank and Joe borrowed the pickup again and headed east on the interstate toward New Berlin.

"Wow, look at that," Joe said, pointing straight ahead. The town of New Berlin had swung into view. "It's a town straight out of a cowboy movie."

The Hardys drove down the single dusty street, taking in the weathered wooden buildings, with the thick green forest as a backdrop. Many of the buildings were abandoned, but others had been newly painted and sported curtains in the windows or long chains of red peppers drying on the wooden porches.

"This must have been some place during its boom years," Frank said as he parked outside a storefront. A sign informed them that the building was the New Berlin Historical Society and Mining Museum. The pleasant, tiny, silver-haired woman inside gave them directions to the Anti-War Alliance headquarters at the opposite end of town.

"I guess we can walk," Joe said as they stepped out into the street again. "The other side of town can't be more than a hundred yards away."

"I can see the headquarters from here," Frank agreed as they started up Main Street. He pointed to the left, to a small, rustic cabin with Victorian gables perched on a slope a little above the town. The brothers walked quickly and turned onto a narrow dirt road that led up the hill past a couple of run-down old barns.

"Let's take a shortcut," Joe proposed, starting across a grassy vacant lot between them and the house. "I can't wait to have a talk with Garth Hudson."

"I'm with you," Frank said, following. "I've had a feeling all morning that Hudson's the key to all that's been going on."

Joe charged across the field, stumbling on the way over the ends of some wooden boards half hidden in the grass. He started across the boards but stopped almost instantly when he heard a loud crack from under him.

"What was that?" Frank called, hurrying to catch up.

"Stay back!" Joe warned.

Before Frank could move another step, the boards beneath Joe collapsed, and he vanished.

"Joe!" Frank raced toward the place where his brother had been. "Where are you?"

"Down here." Frank heard Joe's voice echoing up from a pit in front of him. He got down

53

on his hands and knees to peer into the hole. Joe was dangling from a thick iron rod buried a foot down into the pit. His legs kicked wildly in the empty space below him.

"Hold on, Joe," Frank said, reaching for his brother's hand. As Joe raised one arm toward Frank, the iron rod settled deeper into the pit, dropping Joe farther.

"Whoa!" Joe yelled, swinging free into the opening. "Help! I can't hold on much longer!"

Chapter

6

REACTING INSTANTLY, Frank unbuckled his leather belt and ripped it from his pant loops. He threaded the belt back through the buckle, making a loop in one end. He wrapped the other end around his hand two times. Then he lay flat on his stomach with only his head and shoulders over the pit and lowered the leather belt to Joe.

"Grab this!" he shouted.

Joe stretched for the loop. It was a fraction of an inch beyond his grasp. He strained his arm upward until the tips of his fingers touched the leather.

Frank squirmed forward, giving his brother another precious half inch. Joe grabbed the loop firmly, locking his hand around it.

"I've got it!" he shouted as the iron rod pulled away completely and tumbled into the pit, leaving Joe swinging from the end of the leather belt. He reached up with his other hand to get more of a grip on it. "Pull me out of here," he shouted.

Frank started wriggling backward on his stomach, slowly lifting Joe out. From somewhere behind him he heard shouts, and the sound of someone running.

An instant later, massive arms were reaching past Frank's, grabbing the belt and pulling along with him. Slowly, like a fish on a line, Joe rose from the pit and lay panting on the ground.

"Are you all right, son?" asked the man who had come to Frank's aid. Frank looked up to see a tall, muscular man in a plaid shirt with a long ponytail who was trying to catch his breath. Beside him stood a slightly smaller balding man in a plaid shirt and faded jeans.

"This entire mountain is wormholed with abandoned mine shafts," the second man pointed out. "You're mighty lucky you aren't on the bottom," he added to Joe. "And believe me, it's a long way down."

The first man picked up a flat piece of metal lying near the pit and turned it around. It read: Warning—Mine Pit—Danger!

"Most of the pits have been covered over, but

56

not this one, and somehow the warning sign fell down," he said.

"I'm okay," Joe said, breathing more steadily now. "Thanks for saving my life."

"You boys must be tourists," the first man said. "Locals know better than to walk anyplace they're not familiar with."

"We're looking for Garth Hudson," Frank explained.

The balding man pointed to the cabin on the slope several hundred feet away. "Right up there," he said. "Just stick to the roads when you're in New Berlin."

After thanking the men for their help, Frank and Joe walked carefully back to the gravel road and up to the cabin. When they reached the yard a large black dog bounded around the corner of the house, barking furiously. The front door opened. "Here, Jigs!" a man shouted. "Stop it!"

The speaker stepped outside carrying a rolled-up newspaper and grabbed the dog by the collar. He was tall and lanky, with dark brown hair and a beard.

"That's the protestor who threw the sign at us yesterday," Joe said to Frank as the man swatted the dog on the nose with the newspaper and sent him away.

Frank nodded. "We're looking for Garth Hudson," he said to the man. "I'm Frank Hardy, and this is my brother, Joe."

"I'm Garth," the young man said suspiciously. "What do you want?"

Before Frank could answer, the front door opened again, and a young woman stepped out. Frank recognized her as the woman who had tried to pull Hudson away from their truck the day before.

"Hi," the young woman said, smiling at the Hardys. "I'm Merilou Parsons. Are you looking for the Anti-War Alliance?"

"Yes, in a way," Joe said, glancing at his brother. "We wanted to talk to Garth about—"

"I know what you want to talk to me about. I recognize you from TCI yesterday. This concerns Gentle, doesn't it? The top story on the radio today was about the discovery of his body and the warrant for his arrest."

He glared at the Hardys. "Gentle got what he deserved," he said bitterly.

"Garth!" Merilou scolded. "That's a terrible thing to say. No one deserves to die like that."

"What did you have against Dr. Gentle?" Frank asked Hudson sharply.

"He thought nothing of making nerve gas for TCI," Garth shot back. "Gas that could be used to kill innocent people!"

"Can you prove that?" Frank asked.

"I could if anyone would listen to me!" Garth shouted.

Merilou came down the steps and slipped an arm through Garth's.

"Maybe people would listen," Joe suggested quietly, "if you didn't shout and try to break their windshields."

Merilou blinked. Garth stiffened. "I want you off my property," he ordered, pointing toward the road.

"Garth," Merilou protested.

"I'm not arguing about it. Just get off my property!" Garth turned and stormed back into the house. The door slammed behind him.

Merilou watched him go before turning back to Frank and Joe. "I'm sorry. He's upset. He and Dr. Gentle were very close when Garth worked at TCI. But when Garth lost his job and everything, naturally he felt betrayed."

"Why was he fired?" Frank asked.

Merilou suddenly became self-conscious. "Look, I'd better get inside," she told them abruptly. "I don't know what you want here, but you'd be better off leaving us alone."

The message was clear. Merilou smiled quickly and followed Garth into the house.

"Nice work, Joe," Frank said sarcastically. "That little comment of yours drove Hudson right into the house."

Joe became annoyed. "We weren't going to

get anything out of him, anyway. And besides, it was true—if you go around shouting in people's faces like he does, no one's going to listen."

They started down the gravel road toward Main Street. They were halfway down the hill and walking past a sagging woodshed when Frank abruptly stopped.

"What's up?" Joe asked.

Frank glanced up the hill behind them. The curtains were drawn across the windows in Garth Hudson's house. Frank didn't think Hudson could see them.

"That shed," Frank said. "There's something dark green inside. I caught a glimpse through the window as we came up on it."

The window facing the road was opaque with dust except in one corner, where a pane of glass had fallen away. From where he was standing all Joe could see inside was darkness.

"Let's do this fast," Frank said. He stepped off the road toward a set of double doors on the side. Joe followed silently. The shed was ancient, with gaps between the vertical planks of wood. Frank pressed his eye to one space to peer inside.

He recognized the Jeep immediately by its crumpled left front fender and the missing parking light. He heard Joe give a low whistle and stood back. Joe was peering through a knothole in the other door.

"Keep a lookout," Frank told Joe. "I'll be back in a second."

Frank slipped inside the shed and opened the passenger door of the Jeep. Inside the glove compartment he found the registration papers. The name on the document was Garth Hudson. Now there was no doubt in his mind that Garth had been at Wolf's Tooth Canyon when Dr. Gentle died.

Slipping back out of the shed, Frank said to Joe, "Garth knows a lot more than he's letting on. That's his Jeep all right. My guess is he got in a scuffle with Dr. Gentle at the canyon, and Gentle accidentally fell. We need to talk to Sheriff Wilkins."

"First let's get out of here," Joe said, glancing nervously back toward Garth's cabin. "I'd hate to see Hudson come barreling out of his cabin with a gun."

Frank and Joe hurried back to the pickup truck. They reached Tiffany's house a short time later, but to the Hardys' surprise it was empty.

"Look," Joe said, pointing to the answering machine on the kitchen counter. "There are thirty-six messages. Do you think we should listen to them?"

"Most of them are probably from people who've just heard about her father's death,"

Frank pointed out. "Let's just call the sheriff and Mom and Aunt Gertrude. I want to get the news to Dad."

Frank took out his wallet and removed the card Sheriff Wilkins had given him with the address and phone number of his office in Page, Arizona, which was between Wolf's Tooth Canyon and the Utah border. While Joe checked the refrigerator to put together a late lunch, a dispatcher put Frank through to the sheriff.

"I'm glad you called." Frank heard Sheriff Wilkins's voice rise above the static on the line. "We found something out at Dr. Gentle's autopsy this morning. Seems he wasn't killed the way we thought he was."

Frank listened excitedly as Joe laid out ingredients for sandwiches on the kitchen counter.

"Dr. Gentle was dead before he went over the edge—from a blow to the head." The sheriff's voice was lost in static for a moment. Then it came through again, loud and clear.

"Gentle's death was no accident," the sheriff said. "It was murder!"

THE HARDY BOYS CASEFILES

Chapter

7

"Do you have a murder weapon?" Frank asked. He glanced at Joe, who now stood, bread in hand, waiting to hear the news.

"It might have been a rock," the sheriff said. "If Dr. Gentle was near the edge when he was hit, he might have toppled over into the canyon—or maybe his body was thrown in to cover up the crime. Now, didn't you boys mention that you saw a green Jeep leaving just as you pulled in?"

"That's what I called about," Frank said excitedly. "We found the Jeep this morning. It's in a shed in New Berlin, registered to a guy named Garth Hudson."

"Looks like we'll have to ask this fellow a

few questions," the sheriff said. "New Berlin's not in my jurisdiction. I'll have to call the sheriff there."

After finishing his conversation with the sheriff, Frank hung up and told his brother the news. "Unbelievable," Joe said, clearly stunned. He handed Frank a roast beef sandwich on a plate. "I can imagine Garth knocking Dr. Gentle into the canyon accidentally—he obviously has a serious temper. But murdering him with a blow to the head? Garth doesn't seem like the type."

"He did say Dr. Gentle deserved to die," Frank pointed out as he picked up the phone to call their aunt Gertrude. "And he assumed when you and I showed up that we were there to talk about the murder. It seems to me he has a guilty conscience. Anyway, I'm calling home." He took a big bite of his sandwich and dialed the number.

Gertrude Hardy answered on the second ring. She was delighted to hear from Frank, but his news came as a shock to her. She promised to send a message to their father in Kazakhstan, though she wasn't sure when he'd receive it. Then she said she was worried about her nephews' safety.

"Don't be worried. You should be proud of us," Frank reassured her as Joe sat down at the table to eat. "When we discovered who the green Jeep belonged to, we called the police instead of moving in on him ourselves."

After Frank had spoken to his mother, he joined Joe in looking over one of Dr. Gentle's notebooks.

"These maps of the canyons are incredibly detailed," Joe exclaimed. "He's marked the sites of every ruin and petroglyph, and all the best places to camp."

Frank examined one page. On one side was an ink drawing mapping out a small portion of a narrow slot canyon. The opposite page was covered with tiny, spidery handwriting interspersed with simple sticklike petroglyphs that Dr. Gentle had copied and carefully numbered for location.

"He makes a guess as to what the petroglyphs might mean, and he also describes the details of the natural features surrounding them," Joe said, reading the passages in the book.

As Frank deposited his dishes in the sink, he glanced out the kitchen window to see Tiffany climbing out of Michael Slovik's battered Chevy. As soon as Tiffany shut the door, Michael hit the gas and threw up a spray of gravel as he flew out of the driveway.

When Tiffany entered the kitchen Frank could see that she'd been crying. She seemed to be surprised to see Frank and Joe. After a slight shocked pause she ran and threw her arms around Frank's neck.

"What is it? What's the matter?" Frank asked gently.

"Michael broke up with me," Tiffany told him, pulling back and wiping away her tears. "I told him what happened to Dad, and ten minutes later he was saying he didn't think we should see each other anymore."

"That creep!" Joe said, his face flushed with anger. "What timing! You want me to talk to him for you?"

"No. Thanks, anyway," Tiffany said with a weary sigh. "Obviously, Dad was right—Michael wasn't right for me. I guess I just went out with him because it made Dad so mad. Better to have him mad at me than to have him just ignore me."

Tiffany closed her eyes. "I just wish we'd broken up when Dad was still alive," she said in a small voice. "Now I feel like I have a lot to make up for."

"Tiffany, the sheriff in Page phoned," Frank began. Tiffany turned her attention to him, her expression full of dread. Frank told her the latest development in her father's death, and she took the news as if she'd been dealt a physical blow.

"It just gets worse," she said, biting off a sob. "I—I wish he could be back and we could start all over again."

"Can you tell us anything more about Garth

Hudson?'' Joe said. ''Like what happened to get in the way of his friendship with your father?''

''Garth?'' Tiffany acted wary. ''He was one of Dad's lab assistants at TCI. They used to go on expeditions together, too. Then they started fighting about a year or so ago. Dad never talked about it, really. All I know is that suddenly Garth stopped coming around. I just can't think Garth would—'' She stopped in midsentence and shook her head. ''This is all too crazy.''

''Tiffany, we stopped by your father's office last night and brought home some of his notebooks,'' Joe said. Tiffany was obviously so upset, he had decided to change the subject. ''He sure did love to find petroglyphs.''

''Oh, yeah. We used to play games with them,'' Tiffany remembered fondly. ''When I was little he'd leave me messages in petroglyphs that I'd have to interpret for a scavenger hunt.''

The telephone rang, and Tiffany answered it. ''Frank, it's for you,'' she said.

He took the receiver from her. ''This is Frank Hardy,'' he said.

''Frank, this is Detective Jefferson from the Coconino County police department,'' a voice said. ''I'm calling regarding the Sam Gentle case. Could you and your brother come give us a statement, and bring along those threatening notes you mentioned to Sheriff Wilkins? We'd also like to see Tiffany Gentle if she's able.''

"We'll be right there," Frank replied. Hanging up the phone, he put a consoling arm around Tiffany. "It's tough enough losing your father without having to deal with all this other stuff, too," he said. "Did you get in touch with your aunt this morning?"

"She's out of town on a business trip," Tiffany told him wearily. "But she'll be back tomorrow, and I know she'll drive up here then to help me with—everything."

"Good," Frank said, relieved. "Then would you be able to come with us to the station and give them a statement?"

Tiffany nodded slowly as she thought.

Frank drove Joe and Tiffany to the Coconino County police station just off the interstate, five miles from the exit for New Berlin. Inside, Detective Jefferson, a somber, heavyset man with a walrus mustache, took statements from each of the Hardys. "Now it's your turn, Tiffany," the detective said, turning his dark brown eyes on her.

"We'll wait outside," Frank said to Tiffany. "We need some air."

Dusk had fallen while the brothers were in the police station. As they stepped outside they saw a police cruiser pull to a stop. The doors swung open, and two uniformed officers got out.

Frank froze. Tall, bearded Garth Hudson was

being pulled from the rear seat of the car, his hands cuffed behind him. He shouted angrily as the officers hustled him inside the building. He obviously didn't notice Frank and Joe as he passed.

"He sure didn't go easily," Frank said, staring after him through the closing glass doors.

"Come on," Joe said, tugging at his sleeve. "It was our responsibility to report what we saw."

"I know," Frank agreed. "But it doesn't seem right, somehow." He flashed a strained smile at his brother. "Call it a hunch."

As they continued to wait they saw Merilou Parsons climb out of a car and head for the station. When she saw Frank and Joe she appeared startled, but almost instantly a determined look came over her face.

"I hear you're the boys who led the police to Garth," she said matter-of-factly before the Hardys could even greet her. "I just want you to know Garth didn't kill Sam, no matter what you think."

"Did they arrest him for murder?" Joe asked her.

Merilou shook her head impatiently. "They came out to question him. He got upset and tried to run away, so they brought him in."

Frank frowned. "Well, Garth is innocent until proven guilty."

"I know, but I'm worried." Merilou seemed to forget her anger. "He's been so bitter, there must be dozens of people who've heard him vow to stop Dr. Gentle. And then there were those notes he sent to the doctor. Did you know he'd sent them? And then there's—well—"

"What?" Joe asked simply.

Merilou raised her head, and for the first time Frank realized she was crying.

"Garth did go out to Wolf's Tooth Canyon," she told them. "But Sam Gentle was already dead. Garth found him at the bottom of the cliff, just as you did. He told me that, and I believe him. He was going for help when you drove in. Then he kind of freaked."

"Why did he go there in the first place?" Frank asked.

"When they were friendly, Garth often accompanied Dr. Gentle on his expeditions," Merilou told him. "They started working Wolf's Tooth Canyon together more than a year ago." Merilou nervously looked off into the distance. "He decided to go out there to confront Dr. Gentle about his research at TCI. He figured they'd have privacy, and the two of them could hash out their differences."

"Well, I guess his anger got the better of him, so he picked up a rock and bashed Dr. Gentle in the head with it," Joe said.

Merilou acted truly shocked. "No, Joe. You

70

don't know Garth. He's committed to use no form of violence.''

"What do you want from us?" Frank asked.

"I'll do anything to help clear Garth," Merilou said. "I know he's a bit overenthusiastic as a protestor, but he's really a good person." She turned from Frank to Joe as if debating something in her mind. Then, abruptly, she took an object from her purse and handed it to Frank. It was a black hardcover notebook.

"Garth found this near the body," Merilou said.

Frank flipped to the back of the notebook. The last pages were empty. He paged backward to the final entry. "It's dated yesterday," he announced excitedly. "The day we found his body!"

"Why are you giving us this?" Joe asked. "It's just filled with his findings at his petroglyph sites."

"Not according to Garth. He says that Dr. Gentle always wrote down what he was thinking about different aspects of his life. His handwriting is hard to read, but many of his thoughts are interspersed with his site findings. Something may come from this book. If what Garth says is true about the chemical formula that Dr. Gentle was working on for TCI, then a lot of people could want that formula. And a lot of them just might kill for it. This book might free Garth."

"What exactly is Garth saying about the formula?" Joe demanded.

"That it's a deadly nerve gas that's been designed to look like a herbicide, which is what TCI claims it's developing."

"Why would TCI do this?" Joe asked.

Merilou gave an exasperated sigh. "For the money. People willing to use chemical weapons will pay top price for them. They certainly don't care that they're illegal."

"So you think someone killed Dr. Gentle to steal the disks carrying the formula?" Joe asked skeptically.

Merilou seemed annoyed by Joe's evident disbelief. "I don't know. Maybe Dr. Gentle wanted to make a fast buck. Maybe he had a secret meeting with a buyer at the canyon, but the buyer killed him instead. I mean, has anyone found these missing disks? No," Merilou continued triumphantly. "So someone must have them. And I promise you it isn't Garth. At least talk to him and listen to his side of the story."

When the Hardys didn't respond she said impatiently, "Oh, do what you want. I have to try to see him."

As she started marching toward the police station Joe called out, "Merilou!"

She turned back to him.

"We'll think about it, all right?"

* * *

Soon after Merilou left, Tiffany came out, and the trio drove back to the house in silence. Tiffany was exhausted, and Frank and Joe were both absorbed by the mystery of Dr. Gentle's death.

The house was dark, and a strong breeze was blowing up from the valley, swaying the long, heavy branches of the pine trees over the house.

"We forgot to leave a light on," Tiffany remarked.

Frank parked, and they were walking to the house together when a gust of wind buffeted them. The front door was blown wide open and was banging against the outer wall.

"We didn't forget to lock the door, though," Frank said. He strode forward and reached inside the door frame for the switch. A second later the foyer and the living room were ablaze with light.

Behind him he heard Tiffany give a little cry at the sight that greeted them. Furniture, books, and clothing were strewn everywhere, ripped and torn as if a lawn mower had been driven through them.

The house had been ransacked!

Chapter

8

FRANK, JOE, and Tiffany walked slowly into the house, their eyes taking in every detail of the destruction. Every cupboard and drawer had been emptied onto the floor, and all the upholstered furniture was slashed open. Dr. Gentle's collection of Anasazi pottery lay in ruins.

"We'd better see what's missing," Frank said. "Tiffany, you check where your father kept his valuables."

"I know one thing that's gone," Joe called out from the kitchen after Tiffany had left.

"What?" Frank demanded, rushing to join him. The kitchen, too, had been ransacked. Cupboard doors were open. Food containers and dishes were spilled and smashed onto the counters and floor.

"Dr. Gentle's notebooks." Joe pointed to the table. "We left them there."

Tiffany entered the kitchen from the bedroom wing. Frank could see she was shaken but was fighting to keep her composure.

"Everything's been searched," she said, her voice quavering, "but nothing was taken as far as I can tell."

Frank told her about Joe's discovery. Then Frank showed her the notebook that Merilou Parsons had given them. "This is the only one left now," he said, "and I have a feeling it's the one the thief was looking for."

"The one suspect we can eliminate in this robbery is Garth Hudson," Joe pointed out.

Frank nodded. "Yeah, he has an ironclad alibi," he added grimly, remembering Garth being led into the police station. "Merilou Parsons can be eliminated, too."

"So someone else wants the notebooks," Joe mused. "But who?"

Frank flipped to the last entry Dr. Gentle had made and showed it to Joe and Tiffany. On one page was a hand-drawn map of a small section of Wolf's Tooth Canyon. On the opposite page was a pencil drawing of a pueblo ruin perched in a pocket of rock high up a canyon wall. With precise shading Dr. Gentle had depicted shafts of light flooding into the slot canyon from far above.

"Your dad was an amazing artist," Frank commented.

Tiffany nodded sadly. "I remember how excited he was when he discovered this ruin. It's in a side canyon off the main branch of Wolf's Tooth Canyon. The area had the most wonderful petroglyphs, too."

On the next page the scientist's handwriting was more like a scrawl, as if he had written in haste. He had recorded a campsite on high ground near the Anasazi ruin. Then came a series of strange shapes and stick figures.

"Petroglyphs," said Joe.

"Right," Tiffany told him. She was sounding calmer now. "Dad copies them from the rocks and catalogs them. That's how he wrote his field guide. Usually, he writes all kinds of information below each one, though."

Tiffany took the notebook from Frank, flipped to the beginning of the book, and pointed to several pages of petroglyphs, each one accompanied by a long stretch of her father's handwriting. "See," she said, "like that." She turned back to the last page again.

"What do these petroglyphs mean?" Joe asked.

"No one knows," Tiffany said. "At least not for sure. But a lot of native people and scientists have some pretty good guesses."

"What about these?" Joe pointed to the last

glyphs drawn in the notebook. The first two were stick-figure men shooting bows. The third was a square with a mazelike design inside it. Then there was a spiral with a dark, thick line slashing through it. Beneath it were a few more. First a stick figure of a man, upside down and headless. Beside it was another stick figure, upright and with an enormous pumpkinlike head. Finally there were two more stick figures without bows.

Tiffany was obviously intrigued. "This reminds me of the clues Dad would give me in scavenger hunts when I was little," she said. "I'd have to figure out the meaning of each sign to decode the message."

She disappeared into the living room. Soon she returned with a thick paperback book.

"This is the book Dad wrote," she told Frank and Joe. Opening it to a page near the beginning, she showed the brothers pages filled with little drawings, each labeled with Dr. Gentle's guesses as to their meaning. By matching the petroglyphs in the notebook to similar pictures in the guide, Tiffany and the Hardys began to make some sense of Dr. Gentle's last drawings.

The first and last glyphs of the twin stick men were probably warriors, they decided. The square with the maze inside symbolized a journey. The headless upside-down man depicted a dead man. The pumpkin-headed creature was

77

the god of death. Only the spiral with the dagger-like slash through it remained a mystery.

"It's weird," Tiffany said quietly. "It's like Dad was telling us a story in code."

Frank was curious. "You know your father better than anyone," he said. "What do think the message is?"

Tiffany studied the drawings and thought a moment. Then she pointed. "The two warriors here—maybe that's you and Joe. And the head-less upside-down man may be my father. And this is Death."

"Right," Joe said doubtfully. "And that gets us absolutely nowhere."

Frank closed the notebook and looked around at the ransacked house. "Let's call the police and start cleaning up. We have a lot to do tomorrow."

"Like what?" Joe asked.

"Like pay a visit to Garth Hudson to get his side of the story."

The next morning the Hardys helped Tiffany restore some order to her house. Her aunt Elaine arrived from Phoenix just after lunch to help Tiffany make funeral arrangements. Tiffany told Frank and Joe that she would go to Phoenix that night with her aunt. She'd come back to pack up her things the next day.

Frank and Joe drove to the Coconino County

police station to find that Garth Hudson's Jeep had been impounded. According to Detective Jefferson, crime technicians were going over it with a fine-tooth comb, hoping to find any evidence relating to the murder.

"Is Garth being questioned about Dr. Gentle's death?" Joe asked the somber detective.

"Of course we're questioning him," Jefferson answered. "But we don't have evidence to indict him for murder yet. He's being kept here for resisting arrest and assaulting a police officer—both serious crimes."

The Hardys asked for permission to speak to Garth, and Jefferson agreed. The brothers were ushered into a small room and told to wait. A moment later Garth Hudson strode in angrily.

Garth didn't seem surprised to see the Hardys. The bearded man sat facing them, making direct eye contact. "So you're the two who called the police," he said bitterly. "I want you to know the only reason I agreed to see you is because Merilou begged me to hear you out."

"That's cool," Joe said, trying not to feel guilty. "Do you have a lawyer yet?"

Hudson nodded. "Yes, but so what? You want to ask me something?"

"Why did you and Sam Gentle have a falling out?" Frank asked.

"Let's just say I got to know him better."

"What does that mean?" Joe demanded.

79

"I found out he'd compromise his principles to make chemical weapons—even if it cost innocent people their lives."

Frank frowned. "You claim TCI is making a chemical weapon—some kind of nerve gas. TCI claims to be manufacturing a new herbicide that will revolutionize farming."

Garth laughed bitterly. "It'll revolutionize everything—especially when used by unlawful governments or other forces." He looked at Frank and Joe with an amused expression. "This is way over your heads."

"Try us," Joe challenged.

Garth sighed, then continued. "A year and a half ago, when I worked with Sam at TCI, we were asked to develop a new kind of weed killer. Sholdice had done the preliminary work and gave us a model to work from. It wasn't easy—the formula involved a number of complex chemical processes. So we were deep into the project before I realized what was really going on. Do you have a piece of paper?"

Frank dug a notepad out of his jacket pocket and passed it to Garth. On a blank page Hudson drew two octagons and a pentagon.

"These are molecules," he explained. "The octagons are made of phosphates. The other one is a simple carbon compound."

Hudson drew two lines between the octagons. "This is what we were creating—an herbicide made of two identical molecules bonded together. It's very difficult to join these two molecules, but I discovered that it's very easy to take them apart. All you need is a few basic petroleum products and the right equipment.''

He scratched out the two lines. "Once you separate them you can use another fairly simple chemical process to attach them to this other molecule." He drew a single line from one of the octagons to the pentagon. "And you end up with a very different chemical altogether."

"What?" Joe demanded.

"Nerve gas," he answered flatly.

"In other words," Frank concluded, "you're telling us that the herbicide formula is just a cover for a chemical warfare product that TCI is prepared to sell to the highest bidder—which might include terrorists."

"Bull's-eye," Garth said. "That's the message I've been trying to get across for a year now. But I have no proof—I didn't get away with a copy of the formula, and TCI, of course, denies my claims. Besides, no one really wants to believe that a thing like this is true."

"So what part did Dr. Gentle play in all this?" Joe asked.

"I went to him with it, but he refused to listen to me. The next day he fired me. TCI stands to make a lot of money—illegally. I figure Sam Gentle had to be in on the plan."

"You think Dr. Gentle was making a deal with dirty governments?" Frank asked.

"No, I think Sholdice did, and Gentle went along with it," Garth stated.

"Why did you write threatening notes to Dr. Gentle?" Joe demanded.

Hudson glanced away for the first time, as if he were ashamed. "Sam was my closest friend," he said in a low voice. "Then he stabbed me in the back."

"What were you doing up at the slot canyon the day he died?" Frank demanded.

"I wanted to talk to him. I thought I might find him in Wolf's Tooth Canyon." He sounded as if he desperately wanted Frank and Joe's trust. "I was going to confront him about his research. But I was too late."

Frank took Dr. Gentle's notebook from his pocket. Garth's eyes widened when he saw it. "Where—" he murmured.

"Merilou gave it to us," Frank said. "She said you'd taken it."

Hudson seemed confused. "It was lying behind some rocks on the canyon wall, where his backpack had split open. It seemed important to save his work, so I picked it up. I reacted like a scientist. That's all—I swear."

"What about these?" Frank opened the notebook to the page with the six petroglyph drawings. "Do you have any idea what these mean?"

Hudson moved his finger across the glyphs, reading out the same meanings they had found in Dr. Gentle's guide. "The spiral," he concluded, "usually symbolizes a pathway or a journey, or going through a doorway."

"What about the line through it?" Joe asked.

"I have no idea," he said. He waited a moment before adding, "You guys probably still think I'm the one who killed him, but I'm not."

It was late afternoon by the time Frank and Joe left the jail. "Hudson's story about the chemical weapons could be true," Joe said as they climbed into the truck. "But why would Sam Gentle go along with it? Didn't Dad say he was committed to helping humanity with his work?"

"What if he was tricked into developing this new herbicide?" Frank suggested, turning the key in the ignition. "Then, when he found out it was really nerve gas, he stole the formula to keep it from falling into the wrong hands."

"But Garth said he told Dr. Gentle about it a year ago," Joe pointed out. "And look what happened to him. He got fired."

"Maybe Dr. Gentle didn't believe Garth until a couple of weeks ago—when he wrote that letter to Dad," Frank said.

"Maybe we should drop into the TCI plant on the way back to Tiffany's," Joe suggested.

Frank nodded. "Just to hear Dr. Sholdice's version of reality."

When the Hardys arrived at Titan Chemicals the shift was changing, and workers were streaming out of the plant. The Hardys had to wait until their cars had left the gate before the security guard waved them in.

The parking lot was almost empty. Half a dozen cars were parked near the research labs, but the only car in the visitors' area was a white late-model station wagon. As they walked around to the front of the executive office building Joe saw an expensive European sedan in a space marked for Armand Sholdice. "Good— he's still here," Joe remarked.

They entered the modern office building and went up to the executive offices. The receptionist's area was empty, but as they entered the waiting room Joe saw that the heavy doors of Sholdice's office were open. A man's harsh voice drifted out.

"Thirty thousand bucks, Sholdice. They're your gambling debts, and the boss wants the money now!"

Frank stopped Joe with a quick hand signal. The brothers froze and listened.

"I'm doing the best I can." Sholdice's voice sounded weary and frightened. "But I have to find those disks with the formula before I can get the money to pay up."

As Frank and Joe listened a third voice snarled, "Then you'd better find them soon, pal. You know what happens to folks who don't make good on their debts. They end up dead meat!"

Chapter

9

FRANK TUGGED ON Joe's arm, pulling him
toward the stairs, away from Sholdice's office.
The rest of the second floor seemed deserted,
but the Hardys could still hear muffled shouts
from the office beyond the reception area.

"Thirty thousand dollars in gambling debts,"
Joe whispered. "And who do you figure this
boss is?"

"Let's split up," Frank suggested quickly.
"When the guys threatening Sholdice leave, I'll
follow them. Maybe they'll lead me to someone
we should know about. But I think it's time to
keep an eye on Sholdice as well."

"Sounds like a good plan," Joe agreed. "I'll
hang out here till you get back. I can watch the

building from the trees on the other side of the parking lot. If anyone else drops in, I'll know about it."

Slipping silently downstairs, the brothers hurried from the building and waited in the pickup truck. Less than two minutes later they saw two powerfully built men leave the building. One wore a turquoise jogging suit with thin red bands around the sleeves. The other wore jeans and a brown suede jacket. They both looked mean—and very pleased with themselves.

Frank and Joe ducked down so they wouldn't be seen as the two men got into the white station wagon and drove toward the gate.

"I'm out of here," Frank said, sitting up behind the wheel.

Joe opened his door and climbed down. "Good luck," he said. "I'll meet you back here."

Frank drove the truck to the gate. Running to the far side of the parking lot, Joe took his position among some bushes in front of a group of pines. He was well hidden by the shrubbery but still had a clear view of the glass-walled office building.

As twilight thickened, a full moon began to rise above the San Francisco Peaks, just visible behind the roof of the office building. Fluorescent office lights glowed through the gray-tinted glass, making the interior office as visible as a

87

room in a cutaway dollhouse. Joe watched Sholdice inside his brightly lit office on the second floor. He was hunched over his desk for more than an hour while the lights of Flagstaff came on, glittering in the thin mountain air. Suddenly Sholdice made a frantic string of telephone calls. Then he sat back.

Joe watched as the last line of red faded from the west and a wash of stars began to glitter in the cold night sky. Shivering in his thin jacket, he kept one eye on the gate for any sign of Frank.

Behind the glass wall of his office Sholdice paced back and forth. At one point he took his coat from a closet and laid it across a chair.

He's impatient to leave, Joe thought. He watched as the tall, thin man answered the telephone, listened for a moment, then spoke quickly into it. Abruptly Sholdice hung up the phone and reached for his coat.

Joe knew he had to make a fast decision. Sholdice's car was in its space, sixty feet away. It would be a risk to go along for the ride, but Joe decided he had to take it.

As the lights went out on the second floor Joe raced through the darkness along the edge of the lot and ducked into the shadow cast by the office building. Hunching over to escape the view of the security guard, Joe raced to the luxury sedan. As quietly as he could he opened the back door. The smell of expensive leather wafted out at him.

Joe crept inside and eased the door quietly closed behind him. He flattened himself on the floor behind the front seat and pulled up his dark coat collar to hide his blond hair. A moment later he heard footsteps along the pavement outside hurrying toward the car. The driver's door opened, and a key was turned in the ignition before the door was closed again.

Sholdice must be pressed for time, Joe thought, holding his breath and trying not to make the slightest sound or movement. When the car began to move he slowly let out a lungful of air and just as slowly inhaled. He felt the car slow down as Sholdice called good night to the guard at the gate.

The sedan turned right and soon picked up speed. A few minutes later Joe heard the tires screech as the car circled around what seemed to be a cloverleaf ramp at great speed. Soon the whoosh of semis roaring past told him they were on the interstate.

Slipping his arm out where he could see his watch, Joe kept track of the time that passed until Sholdice left the highway. After twenty-three minutes the car swung in another half circle as it sped down an exit ramp and turned left.

This new road was in poor condition, Joe

noted as he felt the car jolt in and out of potholes. The car maneuvered several tight curves and then started climbing steeply. They were going up a mountainside, Joe realized.

A short time later the car turned onto a rough gravel road. Joe bounced on the floor of the backseat, trying not to make a sound. Suddenly the car slowed almost to a halt, then turned left and lumbered slowly onto another road.

Where are we? Joe wondered as a rock scraped the undercarriage of the car. Branches scraped against the sedan on both sides before it lurched to a stop. To Joe's relief, Sholdice turned off the ignition and got out.

Joe waited, inhaling the smell of woodsmoke as Sholdice's footsteps marched away and a door opened and slammed shut. Joe heard the faint sound of voices from the other side of the door, but they were impossible to understand.

Carefully Joe pushed himself up and peered over the edge of the car window. He saw that he was in a clearing in a pine forest. Ahead of him stood a small cabin.

Quietly opening the car door, Joe slipped outside. The yard was covered with mountain grass. Behind the cabin, rising above the pines, he saw a snow-covered peak glittering in the silver light of the moon. On one side of the cabin, almost hidden in the shadow, he could just make out the shape of another car.

Crouching, Joe ran toward a window of the cabin. He caught a quick glimpse of the profiles of two men sitting at a table in the middle of the room before pressing out of sight against the side of the building. Slowly Joe twisted back and peered again through the glass. One of the men was Armand Sholdice, and he was gesturing angrily at the dark-haired man across the table from him.

Peering at the profile of the other man, Joe gasped. It was Michael Slovik, Tiffany Gentle's ex-boyfriend! On the table between the two was an open briefcase filled with stacks of American currency.

"It's all yours," Joe heard Slovik say to Sholdice in a taunting voice. He slammed the briefcase shut. "Thirty thousand dollars in exchange for the formula."

"I'm still trying to find the disks," Dr. Sholdice assured the young man.

"Trying!" Slovik said angrily. "You were a fool for killing Gentle before you had the formula in hand."

"It was an accident," Sholdice explained pleadingly. "I didn't mean to kill him—just knock him out so I could search his backpack for the disks. He hid them somewhere in that slot canyon—I'm sure of it!"

"What makes you so positive?" Slovik demanded.

"I saw him take the disks," Sholdice answered. "He ran from the building and drove off before I could stop him. So I went to the roof and followed his car in the helicopter. He drove straight to Wolf's Tooth Canyon. By the time I found a place to land and tracked him down, he no longer had the disks. They have to be in that canyon somewhere."

Joe watched Slovik remove the briefcase from the table. Dr. Gentle's stolen notebooks had been hidden behind it. "I went to a lot of trouble to get these back," Slovik snarled. "My boys tore Gentle's whole house apart looking for the last one."

"It doesn't matter. Gentle kept a record of every canyon he visited, and he'd been visiting Wolf's Tooth Canyon for more than a year," Sholdice told him. "One of those books has to have something in it that we can use."

"It didn't help matters when you gave these books to those Hardy brothers," Slovik said.

"I thought I could use them to dig up the missing formula," Sholdice protested. "But all they've done is stir up a lot of trouble."

Joe saw Slovik laugh. "As long as they set up people like Garth Hudson instead of us, they're being a big help."

"The trouble is, they won't stop there," the

older man said miserably. "I have a feeling they'll keep snooping until they find the formula for themselves."

"Don't worry about the Hardys," Slovik said, his handsome face gleaming in the lamplight. "I plan to take care of them—for good!"

Chapter

Chapter

10

FRANK DROVE SLOWLY past the TCI gate with
barely a nod to the security guard. He kept a
careful eye on the white station wagon with the
two men inside. Soon it turned right onto the
access road and headed for the westbound ramp
onto Interstate 40. Frank followed.

Traffic was heavy, but it was easy to pick out
the white car even in the dark, so Frank felt
confident enough to give his quarry a ten-car
lead. From the high vantage point of the pickup's front seat he could keep his eyes on the
station wagon's square taillights bobbing along
in front of him.

The car exited into Flagstaff. Frank slowed
and followed it onto the exit ramp. The station

wagon had entered an industrial neighborhood of ramshackle brick warehouses, grass-filled vacant lots, and scrap-metal yards. A quarter of a mile ahead Frank saw the square taillights turn right at a broken neon sign that read, Happy Dayz Trailer Park.

Frank cruised slowly past the turnoff and peered down the road the car had taken. A dozen battered trailers huddled in the dark among rows of tall pines. Most of the trailers were overgrown with vines and patched-on additions that made them look as if they had been there for fifty years. The white station wagon was the only moving object in sight.

Frank pulled the truck past the turnoff and parked a short distance down the road. He climbed out of the truck and cut across an empty lot toward the trailer park, his back to the passing traffic. A tall hedge lined the park's border, but its tangled branches were thin and brittle, and Frank easily broke through them.

Lights glowed from the curtained windows of several nearby trailers. As Frank padded down the ramshackle street, he tried to stay in the shadows. He hadn't seen which trailer the station wagon had gone to, but he figured it wouldn't be hard to find. Moving silently down the road, he felt almost invisible. This illusion was suddenly shattered as, with a low-pitched growl, a huge rottweiler charged out of the carport of the next trailer.

Trained attack dogs don't bark, Frank thought as he threw up his arms to protect his face from the charging beast. The big black-and-tan dog crashed into him, its eighty pounds knocking him onto the seat of his pants. As Frank reached out for the dog's throat he realized that the dog was no longer attacking. In fact, it was seated on its haunches a few feet away, staring at him as if he were the most foolish creature the dog had ever seen.

Standing up, Frank petted the beast for a moment. "Little late at night to be making friends, isn't it, boy? But I'd rather have you as a friend than be your midnight snack."

Frank continued down the road, glancing back to make sure that the overenthusiastic dog wasn't following him. At the end of the road he spotted the white car parked in front of an old green trailer with paint peeling in patches. Years earlier someone had added a wooden porch to one side, but it was sagging now. The slatted windows were open, but shades had been pulled most of the way down. It seemed to be the only trailer close by that was occupied.

Darting into the shadows beside it, Frank could hear voices from inside. He crept along the outer wall to one of the windows and peered through the narrow space between the bottom of the shade and the windowsill.

"Some setup," the man in the jogging suit said. He sat in the trailer's living room, dealing out a hand of cards. His companion had removed his suede jacket and was popping open a can of soda. "I still can't figure what the boss is up to," the second man said, "Do you know?"

The other man grunted in reply. He seemed more interested in playing cards. Examining his hand, he withdrew two cards and threw them onto the table.

"Think about it," the man drinking the soda persisted. "A couple of years ago he shows up here and hires us to make like loan sharks with Sholdice."

"Sholdice needed the money," the other one said. "Going to Vegas every week, he must have lost a bundle over the years."

"Yeah, I know, but it doesn't make sense," the first man said. "First the boss loans Sholdice all that money. Now he wants to pay the guy the same amount for this formula or whatever it is. I pass," he added, putting his cards facedown on the table. He shook his head. "If he wanted something from Sholdice, why didn't he just buy it in the first place? Sholdice doesn't even know that the person he borrowed from and the person who's going to pay him are the same guy."

Frank saw the second man give his partner an

exasperated look before he swept the cards from the table. "You've got a lot to learn," he said, shuffling the cards. "It's easy to figure out. You borrow from the wrong kind of people and don't pay it back, you can get your legs broken—or worse. Sholdice had something the boss wanted, so the boss set him up. Once a guy is really desperate for money he'll do anything."

Frank watched the man start to deal another hand of cards. The man in the jogging suit leaned back in his chair, his eyes moving toward the window. Frank pulled back against the side of the trailer before he was seen. He heard the man say, "I'm just wondering if there's anything extra in it for us. You know—a way we can collect at both ends, like the boss."

There was a brief silence before Frank heard the other man reply in a stern, angry voice, "As long as we're paid, we're going to mind our own business and play cards."

A telephone rang somewhere at the back of the trailer. Frank heard a weary groan as one of the men stood to answer it. Frank crouched under the window and silently moved down the length of the trailer, following the sound of the footsteps. As he reached the rear window a light went on, and Frank heard the telephone being picked up.

"Yeah, boss?" It was the voice of the man with the suede jacket.

"Two brothers?" Frank heard the man say into the phone.

A cold chill raced up Frank's spine. He pressed closer to the window, listening carefully.

"What's their names?" the man asked. There was a long pause. Then, "No problem, boss. We'll get rid of them—permanently."

Frank heard the man hang up the phone and start back to the living room. Creeping alongside the trailer to the other end, Frank peered under the shade in the living room window in time to see the man put his suede jacket back on.

"Forget the card game," the man said. "The boss wants us to track down a couple of nosy teenagers."

"Oh, yeah?" said the man in the jogging suit. "Who are they?"

"Frank and Joe Hardy," the first man said. "They're probably over at that Gentle's house."

"And when we find them, what do we do?" asked the man in the jogging suit, standing up.

"We kill them," the other one replied.

Immediately Frank felt his feet slide on the wet grass beneath his feet. He went down and slammed against the side of the trailer with a loud thump.

"Someone's outside!" he heard one of the men say. These words were followed by rapid footsteps. Before he could move Frank heard the door open, and the two men raced toward him.

Chapter

11

FRANK ROLLED underneath the trailer. Closing his hands around the steel undercarriage, he pushed his feet against one end and pulled himself up, holding his body above ground level. From the corner of his eye he saw two pairs of feet appear around the corner of the trailer, following the beam of a flashlight.

"You see anyone?" he heard the man in the jogging suit growl.

"Uh-uh," said his partner. "But I sure heard something a minute ago."

There was a long pause. Frank heard the feet pacing through the wet grass. His biceps strained to keep his body off the ground. A trickle of sweat rolled along his forehead and tickled him.

"Ah, it was just the wind," one of the men said.

"I don't know," the other answered suspiciously.

There was another short silence. Frank had to loosen his grasp. The sharp metal edges of the undercarriage were cutting into the palms of his hands. Finally he heard one of the men say, "Check under the trailer."

Frank forced himself to tighten his grip. A moment later he saw the flashlight beam cut across the space beneath him. He knew he couldn't hold out much longer.

"Naw, no one here," the man with the flashlight said. "Just a strong gust of wind slammed against the trailer. You know how it is in these mountains."

"Yeah—I guess you're right." To Frank's ears the voice still sounded suspicious. But the flashlight's beam moved away from him, around to the other side of the trailer. "Let's go take care of those Hardy brothers like the boss asked," the voice added.

Frank waited, perfectly still, as the station wagon's doors opened and slammed shut. The engine was started, and the car drove off. Slowly Frank lowered himself to the ground, his cramped biceps screaming as he relaxed them. Shaking his arms to get the blood circulating, he made his way around the trailer and back through the broken hedge to his parked truck.

It was easy to pick up the white car's trail when he reached the interstate. Keeping his distance, Frank followed again, and when the turnoff for TCI came up the car ahead kept going.

They're heading for the Gentles', Frank thought. He was glad that Tiffany was spending the night with her aunt in Phoenix. He took the exit off the interstate for TCI and a few minutes later approached the cyclone fence surrounding the parking lot.

The lot was empty, and Joe was nowhere to be seen. Frank saw the light on in the security booth at the gate. The lone guard inside appeared to be snoozing. Just then Frank heard the sound of a car's engine and spun around in time to see a taxi pull over to the curb.

To Frank's relief, Joe stepped out and ran up to him.

"Good timing," Joe said, slipping into the passenger seat. "Been waiting long?"

Frank shook his head. "Just got back." He put the pickup in gear and hit the gas. He wanted to get as far from TCI as possible while he and Joe exchanged stories. When the goons found the Gentle home empty, there was no telling where they'd look next.

Frank noticed that his brother was beaming

happily. "I take it you found something out. Where have you been?"

"Slate Mountain," Joe said. "A mile from New Berlin, but on a different road farther down the mountain. I didn't know till I was walking back and saw the highway signs. I hitched a ride back to Flagstaff and grabbed a cab back to TCI, hoping you'd be here."

Joe told Frank about hiding in the back of Sholdice's car and the exchange he'd heard at the mountain cabin.

"Michael Slovik!" Frank exclaimed when Joe identified the man Sholdice had gone to see. "He must be the boss those two thugs were talking about. According to them, Slovik lent Sholdice gambling money until he was over his head in debt. Sholdice thinks he owes the money to gangsters, so he's terrified they're going to collect the hard way."

Joe nodded. "So Michael Slovik comes along and offers him the money he needs if TCI will develop a certain herbicide that can be converted into nerve gas."

"Right! And Sholdice doesn't know it, but he was set up right from the beginning." Frank's eyes widened. "Slovik must have dated Tiffany as a way of keeping tabs on Dr. Gentle's work. Then, when she was no longer useful, he dumped her. No wonder Dr. Gentle had a bad feeling about the guy!"

Joe was grim. "We know Armand Sholdice killed Dr. Gentle and that Michael Slovik ransacked the house and stole the notebooks. All we have to do now is find the missing disks with the formula. My guess is that Dr. Sholdice was right. They're hidden somewhere in Wolf's Tooth Canyon."

Frank glanced at his watch. It was almost midnight. "Is that camping equipment still behind the seat?"

Joe twisted around and rummaged through the packs. "Sure is. We could use more water, though. Why? Do you want to drive up to the canyon tonight? It must be ten miles long, with millions of hiding places."

"I know." Frank smiled calmly. "But we still have that notebook, and those petroglyphs have to be clues to where the formula's hidden. I'd like to get to it before anyone else does."

Soon Frank and Joe were heading north again, trading off shifts behind the wheel. As they drove the moon rotated in a slow arc, its light washing across the stark plains of the Painted Desert, its silver brilliance almost wiping out the stars.

While Joe drove Frank turned on his flashlight and flipped through Dr. Gentle's notebook. Reading the dates of each entry and tracking each hand-drawn section of the canyon on a government-issue map, he was able to plot Dr. Gentle's progress over several months. Frank made a special note of one campsite that Dr. Gentle had noted was above the high water mark in time of flash floods. It would make sense to hide the disks high enough to stay dry, Frank reasoned.

In the wee hours of the morning, with the moon setting on the horizon, Frank turned the pickup onto the road that led to Wolf's Tooth Canyon. The waning moonlight illuminated the jagged black opening of the slot canyon like a river of blood flowing in the bottom of the valley.

"Let's hide the truck," Frank proposed, driving off the trail and into the pines. He parked the pickup, and the brothers climbed out, stretching their legs and breathing the chilly mountain air.

"We can sleep here until sunrise," Frank said, "which won't be long from now."

They unrolled the sleeping bags and spread them out in the back of the truck. Lying down under the stars, Joe listened to the yip and howl of distant coyotes until he drifted into a dream.

It seemed as if only moments had passed when Joe felt Frank shaking him awake. He struggled up through layers of sleep to his brother's voice.

"Joe, it's five A.M.," Frank said. "The sun's coming up. Let's get going."

Joe sat up and rubbed his eyes. In the east a thin white line spanned the horizon. As he watched it began to redden, and the sky above faded from black to purple. "I guess that's what you call the crack of dawn," he said with a sigh.

Frank thrust a plastic bag filled with raisins and nuts at Joe, along with a can of orange juice. "We should take our packs with us," he said, "in case we have to camp overnight at the other end and hike back tomorrow."

"Sounds good to me," Joe agreed. "Do you have any idea where we're going to look?"

Frank nodded. "The canyon's about eight miles long. About six miles into it is the last site Dr. Gentle was exploring—a side canyon, according to his notebook. His drawing indicates pueblo ruins high up in the rock at that spot. We'll look there first."

"So you want us to scour every nook and cranny until we find something—that's your plan?" Joe asked.

Frank shook his head. "I've been thinking about that petroglyph Dr. Gentle drew in his notebook—the spiral with a dagger through it. Garth Hudson told us the spiral could symbolize emergence or a doorway."

Joe's eyes widened. "Or a hiding place!" he exclaimed.

"Exactly," Frank said, nodding. "So let's keep our eyes peeled for something that looks like it—either a spiral petroglyph or some kind of dagger-shaped hiding place."

In the half light of early dawn the Hardys descended the valley to the edge of the slot canyon. Birds warbled in the juniper and piñon branches, and a pair of hawks rode the air currents high above the canyon. Just as the sun began to rise fully above the horizon the Hardys reached the edge of the crevasse.

"Remember to watch out for quicksand," Joe said, gazing at the trail that led down into the darkness.

"I will if you will," Frank murmured automatically. He started down the rough trail, aware that his backpack had changed his center of gravity. Feeling the ground ahead with his foot before each step, he descended slowly and carefully. Several times rocks gave way or pebbles slid beneath his feet.

When they finally reached the bottom of the crack in the earth they paused for a gulp of water from their canteens. Both Hardys were bathed in a fine glow of sweat despite the cool air inside the canyon. Frank threw his head back to gaze up the vertical rock walls. The sun was higher now, and shafts of yellow light flooded into the narrow opening.

"This way." Frank pointed in the direction they'd gone to find Dr. Gentle's body before. They started walking and passed the site less than a minute later. The dry gravel creek bed was disturbed by dozens of boot prints from the rescue workers. Just beyond the spot the prints ended—except where small sections of Dr. Gentle's trail survived.

By ten o'clock Frank estimated they had walked three miles. He craned his neck up for the hundredth time to gaze at the light filtering down from above. It shifted and changed every moment, highlighting various colors in the cliff layers. As the sun climbed higher, sunbeams occasionally hit the canyon floor.

"Want to take ten?" Frank suggested, noticing that Joe's face was red from exertion. He started unbuckling the canteen from his belt.

"Sure—or fifteen," Joe said, dropping his pack with a sigh of relief. "I must not be in as good shape as I thought. I'm worn out already."

Frank slugged back a mouthful of water and handed the canteen to Joe. "It's the high altitude," he explained. "The air here has less oxygen than that in Bayport. You breathe in less oxygen, so you get tired faster."

Joe tilted his head back, raising the canteen

to his lips. Just then Frank heard a strange noise—a heavy thunk from somewhere above them. Then he felt gravel beginning to pelt his head.

Frank looked up just in time to see enormous rocks crashing down the sides of the canyon. The rocks were bouncing off the walls and one another with tremendous force and speed. They were falling straight toward the Hardys!

Chapter

12

FRANK RAMMED Joe against the cliff and used his body to protect his brother. The rocks clattered and smashed against outcroppings and ledges, then crashed heavily into the gravel creek bed barely five feet from them.

A moment of silence followed as a cloud of dust rose into the air. Shaken, Joe pushed his brother away. "Thanks for the rescue, Frank, but I probably could have done it myself," he said tensely.

Frank was gazing up at the narrow line of blue high above them. Birds—swallows, probably—darted back and forth across the opening.

"That was an accident, wasn't it?" Joe asked, following Frank's line of vision. "Probably just erosion or something natural like that."

"I hope so," Frank muttered. He looked at Joe. "Let's keep going."

Joe knew when to avoid arguing with his brother. He shouldered his backpack and followed Frank deeper into the slot canyon. As they walked Frank compared every twist and turn with the drawings the scientist had rendered. The drawings were remarkably accurate. But somehow he no longer felt reassured.

"What is it?" Joe asked in a low voice when Frank stopped suddenly, staring up at the rim of the canyon again.

Frank shook his head. "I thought I saw a shadow against the rock up there—as if someone were walking along the edge."

Joe peered suspiciously at the crack of light along the roof of the canyon. "You think someone's following us? You think that's what caused the rock slide?"

"I don't know," Frank said. "Let's just keep our eyes and ears open."

The Hardys found the first petroglyphs exactly where the notebook said they would be—on a huge slab of flat, reddish rock against the canyon wall. Frank approached the strange drawings of one-eyed people, birds, animals, squiggles, and zigzags with awe. "It's like a giant newspaper carved in rock," he said. He pointed to two stick figures with bows. "The warrior twins!"

Joe nodded. In another area there was a number of long, wavy lines. Joe took the notebook from Frank and flipped through it. "According to Dr. Gentle, these lines are a map of the canyon," Joe said. He passed the notebook to Frank.

Joe peered closely at the wavy-lines petroglyph, puzzled over whether it could be a map. Gradually, however, he could make out the narrow channel of Wolf's Tooth Creek. The other lines, he realized, marked the height of the canyon walls.

"A topographical map!" Joe exclaimed. "A thousand years old."

"The people who made this must have been pretty smart," Frank commented.

Joe nodded. "That's for sure. I guess they used this place to—"

His words were cut off by a roaring like thunder. Frank and Joe instantly lifted their heads at the noise.

"Boulders!" Frank shouted, flattening himself against the rock wall beside Joe. The canyon wall protruded slightly just above their heads, so the rain of stones bounced off it and rolled down inches from the Hardys' stunned faces. Once again boulders crashed into the canyon floor, and again there was sudden, eerie silence after they fell.

"That was no accident," Joe said grimly. "That was enemy action."

Frank flipped through Gentle's notebook until he found a map and notes for the area in which they stood. "I thought so," he muttered, tracing his finger along the hand-drawn map.

"What?" Joe demanded, glancing anxiously overhead.

"He's marked an alternative route out of here. It's a side canyon about half a mile down," Frank said in a low voice.

"You think we should climb to the surface, circle around, and try to surprise whoever attacked us?" Joe asked.

Frank shook his head. "I think we should split up. I'll climb to the surface. Give me an hour while you move up the canyon to the far end. Then make noise so that whoever is up there will know you're still here. I'll try to come up behind him."

"How do you know there's not more than one up there?" Joe challenged his brother. "It could be those two guys who work for Michael Slovik."

"Because if there were, a lot more rocks would be coming down at us." Frank gestured toward the boulders that had fallen. There were three, each about the size of a pumpkin. "The rocks fell from only one spot, so my guess is that one person is stalking us. Anyway, I'll have the advantage of surprise."

"When you find him, push him over the

edge," Joe muttered, only half joking. "That'll stop his little rock slides."

Frank chuckled. "Just don't take any dumb chances while you're being the decoy."

"Don't worry about me," Joe said, shooting Frank a cheery grin.

Keeping a careful eye on the cliffs overhead, the brothers continued down the canyon. "Stay close to the walls," Frank told Joe. "It reduces our odds of being seen."

By the time they had hiked another half mile the sun was almost directly overhead. Its light cast a thin white line down the gravel bed. Frank saw a shadow flash across the line and immediately slammed his brother back against the wall.

"What happened?" Joe whispered. Frank signaled him to keep quiet. They listened carefully but heard only the deep, almost clammy silence. Frank released Joe, and the two moved cautiously forward again. A few minutes later they reached the entrance to the side canyon. It was even narrower than the fissure they had been following—barely wide enough at shoulder height for a person to pass through.

"Okay, get out of here," Joe murmured as Frank checked the notebook again, then handed it to him. "Hurry up—I'm going to be making a lot of noise soon."

"I should be at the top in about fifteen minutes," Frank reminded him. "Catch you later."

With a thumbs-up sign Joe watched his brother start up along a narrow cleft between two boulders. Then he turned and continued his hike down the slot canyon, purposely kicking stones out of his way and glancing up at the crack of light snaking overhead. As he plunged deeper into the narrow space between the two rock walls he twice caught the flicker of a shadow in the line of light that filtered through to the canyon floor.

Someone's watching me, Joe realized as a chill went up his spine. I might as well keep him entertained, he decided. Whistling softly, he continued around and over a jumble of rocks. Just as he stepped down onto the ground again he heard a loud crack. Looking up, he saw another boulder bouncing down the chasm, ricocheting from side to side.

"Uh-oh," Joe said out loud, glancing quickly to his right and left. There was nowhere to go but straight ahead.

As the boulders sent dust and tiny shards of rock like rain into the canyon, Joe ran, the heavy pack bouncing on his back. Just as the boulders crashed to the ground behind him Joe stumbled into a slightly wider section in which the stone walls, eroded by centuries of rain, undulated like waves. Above, the sky was almost hidden by stone protrusions jutting out from the high walls.

For a few minutes, at least, Joe felt safe. He caught his breath and took several sips from his canteen, swirling the water around his dry mouth.

At least the guy's still following me, he thought, hoping that Frank had made it out of the side canyon. He looked down the canyon, noting the unprotected places where falling rocks could hit him. His gaze stopped on a group of shapes and lines on a smooth rock face twenty feet away. More petroglyphs! he realized.

Moving closer to inspect the drawings, Joe saw that they were similar to the ones the Hardys had found earlier. The two stick-figure warriors were here again, this time without bows. A series of small circles had been drawn around their heads. Joe wondered what the circles meant.

From his new vantage point Joe noticed another branch canyon leading to the right, barely wide enough for a person with a backpack to enter. The walls on both sides of the cleft were covered with hundreds of rock art designs, including the pumpkin-headed god of death, drawn upside down. It's like a warning, Joe thought. Do not enter.

Taking Dr. Gentle's notebook from his backpack, Joe flipped to the second-to-last map the scientist had drawn. Tracing with his finger his progress along the side canyon, Joe found the tiny cleft with the petroglyphs clearly marked. The cleft led to the pueblo ruins on the cliff that Frank and Joe had been heading for—the last site Dr. Gentle had explored.

Joe glanced up quickly. The extremely narrow, twisting walls of the cleft protected him from large falling boulders. Satisfied, Joe squeezed inside. The petroglyphs continued for a short distance, then ended at an abrupt curve. Joe turned the corner and stopped.

Before him the canyon walls parted in an opening nearly twenty feet wide and a hundred feet long. High up in a hollow in one red rock wall Joe spotted a group of imposing thousand-year-old stone ruins perched on the narrow rock terraces. They looked exactly as Gentle had illustrated them in his notebook—crumbling walls, fallen roofs, gaping doorways and all. Shallow rectangular slots, chiseled into the rock wall to form a kind of stairway, led up to the ruins from the canyon floor. In the strange light filtering into the canyon the ruins were ghostly, as if invisible spirits lurked within.

Joe spotted something else—a giant petroglyph of a spiral on the wall below the ruins. Running vertically through the center was a long, thin dagger of darkness—a space where the rock had split apart!

Without hesitating, Joe climbed the ancient

steps until he reached a spot half a dozen feet to the right of the petroglyph. Flattening himself against the cliff, he began to inch toward the spiral, digging his fingers and toes into tiny nooks and crannies in the face of the rock. Finally he reached the crevasse.

The crack in the rock was completely dark, but by stretching sideways Joe could just make out a small square object deep within. Glancing up one last time and seeing no one on the surface above him, he reached deep inside and pulled the object out.

It was a small box sealed with waterproof tape. Joe angled it to let the light catch the words written on it. In Dr. Gentle's spidery writing the box was addressed to Frank and Joe Hardy! Joe closed his eyes for a moment and grinned. There was no doubt in his mind—these were the the missing disks with the formula!

Unwilling to take the time to remove the waterproof tape, Joe shoved the box into his backpack. The side trip had already cost him precious time. By his estimate it was another two miles to the end of the canyon where he and Frank would link up—with or without their attacker as prisoner.

Climbing down from the rock wall, Joe jogged as quickly as possible back to the main canyon. Though he kept an eye out for falling rocks, his attacker seemed to have disappeared. Once he thought he heard the faint whir of a distant motor or machine. When he stopped to focus on the sound, it was no longer there. Good, he thought, hurrying along the canyon floor. That means Frank must have nabbed our guy.

It was late afternoon when Joe reached the end of Wolf's Tooth Canyon. An old rock slide had sent slabs of limestone into its narrow tip. He could see a trail winding steeply upward, curling around megaliths of broken rock. As Joe scrambled over narrow ledges and broad rock faces he listened for any sign of Frank, but he heard none.

Finally Joe reached the rim and stood on a windswept plateau. A thin forest of pine and scrub oak grew almost to the rim of the canyon. A sudden, jarring screech caused Joe to spin around. He saw an immense crow, its enormous wings flapping mightily as it lifted off from the top of a pine and flew away.

Breathing again, Joe stepped back from the canyon's edge and began removing his backpack. Just then he noticed a glint of metal through the trees.

He peered closer. It was a helicopter parked in a clearing!

"We meet again, my friend," a threatening voice behind him said.

Joe spun around to face Armand Sholdice.

The man held a gun aimed directly at him. "Where's your brother?" he demanded.

Joe gestured back toward the slot canyon. "He's coming. He'll be up any second."

"And I'll be ready for him," Sholdice said. "Now hand over those computer disks." When Joe hesitated he snarled, "Hurry up! I know you have them. I was watching from up here when you found them in that hole in the rock."

Joe knelt beside his backpack and undid the clasps. Praying for time, he slowly took out the small box.

"Throw it on the ground there!" Sholdice pointed his gun at a spot between them. The man's eyes were gleaming, riveted on the box. Joe tossed the box to the ground.

Sholdice visibly relaxed and gave Joe a smile with no joy. With his gun he gestured to the rim of the canyon ten feet away.

"Start walking," he instructed. *"Backward."*

Joe swallowed and glanced behind him. It was at least thirty feet to the bottom of the canyon at this point—a three-story drop to a hard rock floor. Sholdice lowered the barrel of his handgun and fired. The ground in front of Joe's feet exploded, and he felt shards of rock nick his face and arms.

"Keep going!" Sholdice yelled, his finger stiffening on the trigger of the gun. He raised the barrel. "The next bullet isn't going to miss!"

Chapter

13

"I'M WALKING!" Joe yelled as Sholdice extended his leveled arm and aimed the gun at Joe's chest.

Joe stepped backward again, first one foot, then the other. Carefully he measured each pace, visualizing the distance—and the time—that he had left before he fell to his death.

Suddenly he saw movement in the trees behind Sholdice. Frank Hardy flew into the open from his hiding place behind some low shrubs, tackling Sholdice at the knees and bringing him down. Joe threw himself to the ground just as the gun fired.

The bullet went wild, well over Joe's head. The force of Frank's tackle knocked the gun from Sholdice's hand, and it sailed through the air and disappeared into the canyon.

Frank jumped onto Sholdice's back, wrestling him flat. His opponent struggled to free himself until Frank pinned his arms to the ground. Then Joe helped Frank pull the tall, middle-aged man to his feet. Sholdice's face was red, and his lips were set in a thin line. Frank twisted his arms behind his back and kept a firm hold on them.

"You want to start talking now?" Frank asked him, "or wait until the police get here?"

Sholdice said nothing.

"I found this where Dr. Gentle left it," Joe explained to Frank, ripping the thick tape from the box to reveal a sturdy plastic case. Just as he had known, it was filled with computer disks. There were also several sheets of paper folded in the box. Sholdice's eyes widened.

"Is this what you've been looking for?" Joe demanded.

Sholdice curled his lip. His eyes remained glued to the box in Joe's hands.

"There are a lot of things we already know," Frank told him. "We know you killed Dr. Gentle and threw his body off the cliff."

Sholdice flinched, but he said nothing.

"Tell us what Titan Chemical is really making," Joe said to him. "Agricultural products— or nerve gas for chemical warfare?"

"It depends on who's paying for it and how badly they want it," Sholdice said with a sneer.

"How badly does Michael Slovik want it?" Joe countered.

For an instant fear flashed in Sholdice's eyes. "Slovik is a dangerous man," he told them. "Don't think you can stop him."

Joe looked across the grassy slope to where the helicopter was parked, almost hidden behind a thicket of scrub and pines. "I'll use the chopper radio to get the police," he told Frank, jogging off in that direction.

Joe found the helicopter equipped with a cellular telephone as well as a radio, and he was soon able to get in touch with a state trooper detachment. He asked to be put in touch with Sheriff Wilkins. Wilkins was out on patrol, so Joe gave his story to the dispatcher instead.

"Sit tight," the state trooper told him. "We'll have someone up there right away."

Joe returned to the edge of the canyon. Frank had tied Sholdice's hands behind his back and made him sit on the ground. Sholdice appeared tired and defeated, but Joe knew that he was still as mean as a rattlesnake and just as dangerous.

"I'm going back into the canyon to get the gun," Frank said. "It has his fingerprints all over it. I want to give it to the police."

"The trail is slippery," Joe pointed out.

Frank nodded. "I'll be careful." He started

down the rough trail and soon disappeared between two slabs of rock. Joe waited in silence, keeping a sharp eye on Sholdice until Frank returned twenty minutes later. "Did you find it?" Joe called from where he sat on the hard ground.

Frank nodded. "It's in my backpack," he said. "I dumped out a plastic bag of trail mix and wrapped the gun in the bag."

"Trail mix—that sounds good," Joe said as Frank joined him facing Sholdice. "Let's eat while we're waiting for the cops, okay?"

"There's not much to eat." Frank swung his pack around and opened it from the top. "But I guess even granola is good when you're starved."

The brothers offered their captive a share of their rations, but he declined with an angry shake of his head. Frank and Joe had barely finished when Joe noticed the twin glow of headlights moving over a nearby hillside. The sun had begun to set, and the sky behind it was a dusky rose.

"That must be the state troopers," Joe said, standing up and pointing. He grabbed Frank's flashlight from his backpack and aimed it at the vehicle, flicking the beam on and off.

A few minutes later a Land Rover with a state trooper's crest on the door panel lumbered over the rocky terrain past the helicopter and came to a stop at the edge of the canyon. To Frank and Joe's relief, Sheriff Wilkins got out, along with another officer.

"I hear you have a murder suspect for me," Wilkins boomed as he stepped out, glancing from the Hardys to their unhappy prisoner. "I'm obliged to you boys for making my job a lot easier."

Frank and Joe turned Sholdice and the gun over to the police. While the other trooper handcuffed Sholdice and led him to the Land Rover the Hardys briefed Wilkins on the events of the past couple of days.

"Do you know where we can find this Slovik fellow?" Wilkins asked.

Joe shrugged. "He has a cabin on Slate Mountain. I think I could lead you there, but I don't have an address and couldn't tell you the names of the roads to take."

Wilkins nodded slowly. "It's not in my jurisdiction anyway," he told them. "I'll talk to the people down in Flagstaff and get them on it."

Frank and Joe watched the sheriff return to the Land Rover to use the police radio. A few moments later he called back to them, "I'll drive you boys around the canyon to your truck so you can get back to Flagstaff and go straight to the police there. Ask for Captain Dixon. They're waiting for you to lead them to Slovik's cabin."

"What about this?" Joe asked, holding up the

box of computer disks. "It's the formula that Dr. Gentle was accused of stealing."

Sheriff Wilkins studied the box for a moment, apparently considering a course of action. Finally he looked Joe in the eye. "As far as I'm concerned, I'm working on a murder case. The police in Flagstaff were investigating that other business."

By the time Wilkins drove Frank and Joe around the mountain and back to the slot canyon's trailhead, dusk had fallen, and the sky had turned a deep, dark purple. Frank and Joe climbed into the red pickup, waved goodbye, and started back to Flagstaff while the sheriff took Sholdice to the county jail. By the time they reached the Painted Desert the moon had cast its cold light across the landscape.

"Tiffany was supposed to drive up from Phoenix today, wasn't she?" Frank asked.

Joe nodded. "This afternoon, I think. She could still be at the house. Maybe we should give her a call and let her know the latest development."

"Exactly what I was thinking," Frank said. "Especially since her ex-boyfriend is still on the loose."

Frank pulled over and made the call from a pay phone outside a café. The phone rang half a dozen times before the receiver was picked up.

"Hello? Tiffany Gentle speaking."

"Tiffany, listen. Garth Hudson is innocent," Frank said. "The police have arrested the person who really killed your father. It was his boss, Armand Sholdice. And we found the missing formula in Wolf's Tooth Canyon." He heard a click on the line, then Tiffany's voice again.

"Th-that's great, Frank," she said without enthusiasm. Her voice seemed awkward and distant. "I'm glad it's all over."

"Tiffany?" Frank frowned. "Is everything all right?"

A muffled scream came over the telephone, then sounds of a struggle and a loud clunk as the receiver fell to the floor.

"Tiffany?" Frank repeated into the phone. "Tiffany!"

Frank heard the receiver being picked up— and then the voice of Michael Slovik. "Hey, Frank, good to hear you found my property. I'm going to have to take Tiffany away for a while, but don't worry—I'll be in touch with further instructions. After you hand those disks over to me I'll let Tiffany go. But if you don't, you'll never see her again!"

Chapter
14

JOE KNEW something was wrong the instant he saw his brother's face. Frank told him about the telephone call. "We have to tell Captain Dixon," he finished.

"Wait a second," Joe said. "We have a surprise for Slovik. I *know* where his cabin is."

"You're right," Frank said. "We can stake out the cabin and grab him if he takes Tiffany there."

Joe nodded. "It's on our way to Flagstaff. Let's check it out."

Joe directed Frank up the winding roads of Slate Mountain, remembering the turns from his ride in the back of Sholdice's car and checking his watch for the timing.

"That's it!" Joe said, pointing to a dirt road into the forest. "His cabin's up there."

Frank hid the pickup in the trees beside the road. Then he and Joe walked the rest of the way to the cabin. There were no cars parked outside of Slovik's cabin and no lights on inside. "You think Tiffany's in there?" Joe whispered to Frank.

The older Hardy shrugged. "I guess we should—"

Before he could finish they heard a car behind them. Moving quickly, the Hardys concealed themselves in the edge of the forest.

Slovik's battered Chevy pulled into the clearing and stopped. Slovik and his two henchmen got out. Frank and Joe watched as Slovik reached inside and dragged Tiffany from the backseat. Her hands were tied behind her, and her eyes were wide with fright.

Joe was ready to launch himself at the kidnappers when he felt Frank's hand on his shoulder holding him back. Frank made his hand into the shape of a gun, then pointed at the three men. Joe understood—what could he and Frank do against three men who were probably armed?

"No hard feelings, Tiffany," Slovik gloated, "but I must have those computer disks from your friends."

Joe could see her glaring defiantly at her ex-boyfriend. Slovik patted her cheek. "You were

129

my insurance policy, Tif. You helped me keep an eye on your father while he worked on my formula. I'm sorry it hasn't worked out better for us.''

While Slovik taunted Tiffany his men opened the trunk and unloaded jugs of water, knapsacks, and old-fashioned kerosene railroad lanterns. Slovik pushed Tiffany roughly ahead of him into the pine forest behind the cabin. The two other men followed with the equipment and flashlights.

Frank and Joe moved stealthily around the edge of the forest until they reached the trail Slovik had used. The brothers followed slowly on the uncertain terrain.

Abruptly the flashlight beams disappeared, leaving the forest in utter darkness.

''Now what?'' Joe whispered. Neither of them dared turn on their own lights for fear of being detected.

''Let's sneak up,'' Frank suggested.

They picked their way carefully up the trail, keeping to the shadows along the edge. The trail curved, and they saw a great black hole in the side of the mountain—an old mine shaft!

''We've got to get Tiffany out of there,'' Joe whispered.

''Slovik's not going to do anything to her until after he contacts us about the formula,'' Frank pointed out.

"So what should we do?" Joe asked. "Go for the police? We could end up with a dangerous hostage situation—and Tiffany could get killed."

"I've got it," Frank whispered, turning to face Joe. "Remember when you fell down that open shaft in New Berlin? Those guys who pulled you out told us Slate Mountain is riddled with old mine shafts. Maybe we could find another entrance, sneak up on the kidnappers, and free Tiffany ourselves."

"How would we find another entrance?" Joe asked, keeping his voice low.

Frank thought for a moment. "There's that historical society and mining museum in New Berlin," he suggested. "I bet they have some kind of map of the tunnels in this mountain. They'd have to—for safety's sake if nothing else."

Joe nodded. "Sounds good to me. Let's go for it."

The Hardys quietly made their way back to the pickup and down to New Berlin. A few windows on Main Street were lit, but the building housing the New Berlin Historical Society was dark.

"What now?" Joe asked, worried.

"Let's try Merilou Parsons," Frank suggested. "Maybe she'll know who to wake up."

The brothers drove to the cabin on the hill, their hopes rising when they saw lights in the windows. When Joe banged on the door Garth Hudson answered.

"What do you want?" Hudson demanded.

"We need some help," Joe said quickly as Frank joined him on the front porch.

Garth hesitated. "Let them in," Merilou called from behind him. Garth opened the door wider, and the Hardys stepped inside the house.

"If it's Gentle's murder you've come about, I'm no longer a suspect," Garth told them stiffly. "They let me out this evening."

"We know you didn't murder Sam Gentle," Joe told him. Breathlessly he told Garth and Merilou what had happened.

Garth seemed stunned when Joe had finished. "Sam Gentle never did like Slovik," he said.

"Look, we need to know if there's another way into that mine," Joe said urgently. "Can you help us?"

Merilou nudged Garth. "Of course," Garth answered quickly. "There's almost certainly another entrance. The problem is, it would be incredibly dangerous. Wood supports rot, and the tunnels have collapsed in places. Even if we found a route it might not be passable, and if we try, we might bring the whole mountain down on our heads."

"We're not asking you to go with us," Frank said. "Just help us find a way."

"The historical society keeps a bunch of old mine charts for emergencies," Merilou said.

Garth reached for the phone. "I'll call Sylvia, the woman who runs the museum."

When Garth hung up he grabbed his coat. "Sylvia's meeting us over there."

By the time the Hardys, Garth, and Merilou arrived at the old frame building on Main Street, its windows were filled with light. The tiny silver-haired woman the Hardys had met on their first trip to New Berlin let them in and led them to a huge stack of oversize books in the center of the room.

"The collection isn't complete, but maybe you'll find the part you're interested in," she told them.

Frank opened one of the large bound books. The yellowing pages were covered with rows of numbers and included detailed layouts of intricate, interlacing tunnels. Frank groaned. This could take forever, he thought.

"Don't despair," Garth said. He unrolled a modern government-issue topographical map that showed the contours of Slate Mountain on a large scale.

"Let's start with the surface," Garth suggested. He pointed to the village of New Berlin, a cluster of tiny black squares strung along a red line marking the road. "This symbol that looks like crossed pickaxes represents mine entrances."

"Cool," Joe said. "They're all over the mountain!"

Garth nodded. "Slate Mountain is like a giant anthill filled with tunnels and holes. First let's figure out where Slovik's cabin is."

Frank traced his finger along the road from New Berlin to the highway, then found the other road that led up the mountainside. Halfway along the concentric lines that marked the rising slopes he saw a small black square. Not far from it was another crossed pickax symbol.

"There," Frank said, certain it was the shaft where Tiffany was imprisoned. Hudson read off the two numbers that marked the mine's position on the map.

"As the crow flies, it's less than a mile from here," Joe observed.

"Straight over the top of Slate Mountain, if you're any good at climbing," Merilou commented. "And I don't recommend it at this time of night."

Garth shuffled through one of the big books on the table and stopped. "This is a chart of the mine near Slovik's cabin." he said. "It looks like it's just a narrow side shaft that leads into several chambers. Those chambers then lead to the main tunnel."

Garth found some paper and a pencil and

quickly sketched a simplified map. "It's about half a mile down the road from here," he told Frank and Joe. "There's a cyclone fence around it to keep people out, but we can climb it."

"What do you mean 'we'?" Frank asked.

"I'm going with you," Garth told him. Before Frank could object he added, "Look, I've been down in parts of that mine, so I know what to expect. Besides, I owe it to Tiffany—and Sam Gentle."

Frank nodded. A third hand—especially an experienced one—would be helpful. He turned to Merilou. "Can you call the police and lead them to Slovik's cabin?" he asked her. "Let's hope that by the time they get there we'll have Tiffany back, plus a few prisoners for them."

"Or else," Joe said ominously, "we'll need their backup real bad."

Garth persuaded Sylvia to lend them three steel miners' helmets from the museum's collection. Then he and the Hardys stopped at his house to pick up canteens of water and several coils of rope. Joe drove the pickup through New Berlin and out onto the far side of Main Street. Garth directed him to a paved road that ran east along a narrow plateau, following the contours of the mountain.

"Slow down," Garth said a few minutes later. The truck's headlights picked out a chain-link fence topped with barbed wire in a field between the road and the mountain. "We'll have to climb the fence," he said.

Joe pulled the truck off the road and parked behind a clump of juniper shrubs. Moonlight guided them through high, wet grass to the fence. Beyond it several old buildings of weathered wood had collapsed, their shingled roofs buckled in two like broken backs. Behind them the craggy mountainside rose several hundred feet. In its side, hewn into solid rock, was the entrance to the mine, a dark square big enough to drive a pickup through.

Ignoring the No Trespassing sign on the fence, Frank started climbing, balancing delicately at the top to avoid the barbed wire. When he was sure he was clear he pushed hard and swung free, landing with a thud on the other side.

Garth followed quickly, and then Joe. After Joe had landed, all three switched on their flashlights and headed for the mine.

The rough stone walls of the tunnel led straight into the mountain, far beyond the beams of light. Cautiously Frank and Joe followed Garth. The air in the tunnel smelled metallic and felt cool and damp against their skin.

Garth paused a moment, scanning the map he had made. "This is the main tunnel," he told them. "We go straight through it for half a mile before we turn off."

"Whew," Joe said. "We'll practically be in the middle of the mountain."

"Almost," said Garth.

Joe soon realized that compared to the hike in Wolf's Tooth Canyon, this trek was easy. The floor of the mine shaft sloped downward at a gentle angle, leading the trio deeper into the earth. They reached the turn and entered the narrower branch tunnel, where the ceiling sometimes dipped so low they had to stoop to pass. Joe noticed that the wood struts holding the tunnel up were decayed by insects and rot. Many of them sagged dangerously. In one place the ceiling had collapsed, and Garth and the Hardys had to struggle over the debris on their stomachs.

"We're very close," Garth whispered half an hour later. "We have to be very quiet now."

They had walked only another twenty feet when Joe noticed a faint light in the tunnel ahead. He stopped and immediately switched off his flashlight. Frank and Garth saw the light and followed suit.

Garth and the Hardys deposited their flashlights, canteens, and ropes on the floor and moved slowly toward the glow, running their hands along the wall to guide them. As they drew closer they heard Tiffany's voice ringing in the small chamber at the tunnel's end.

"There's no way you'll get away with this."

Joe's pulse raced as he heard the terror in her voice. "Frank and Joe must have called the police by now. It's only a matter of time before they find me."

"You think they'll look in here? You're dumber than I thought, kid," came the gruff reply.

As they inched closer Frank glanced back at Joe and nodded. Joe understood—the speaker was one of Slovik's henchmen. As they neared the entrance to the chamber Frank silently pressed his back against the wall. Garth and Joe did the same, facing him. Invisible in the darkness, the three listened as the pair inside the chamber argued.

"My father worked his whole life to save lives with his chemicals," Tiffany was saying, her voice unsteady. "If you think I'm going to let you use a formula of his to kill people, you're crazy. I'd rather die!"

"Sounds like a good idea," said her guard, sounding bored. "There'll be one less witness to tell stories to the cops."

Joe shifted uncomfortably against the damp tunnel wall. He wished he could just run in and rescue Tiffany, but there was no telling whether her guard was armed or not. He moved a couple of inches closer to the doorway when suddenly his foot struck a small rock, sending it flying into the room.

"What was that?" Joe heard the guard say as the rock clattered against the floor of the chamber. "Mike, is that you?"

The chamber filled with an ominous silence. Joe's heartbeat pounded in his ears.

Suddenly the tunnel was flooded with light as the man in the jogging suit entered from the chamber. "Who's there?" he shouted. Joe stared—he was face-to-face with Tiffany's abductor!

Chapter

15

JOE TOOK A step forward and threw his fist hard into the guard's jaw. The man tilted sideways. Eyeing Joe with shock and horror, he tried not to stumble and fall. Frank stepped from the other side of the opening and grabbed the oil lantern while Joe swung again, connecting in the same place.

The man's knees buckled slowly. He keeled over and sprawled flat.

"I can't believe you guys," Tiffany said as Frank and Joe rushed to release her. She was sitting, tied to a rickety wooden chair. Her face was streaked with dirt, and her eyes shone with relief. "How did you know where to find me?" she asked, pulling the loosened ropes from her arms.

"Garth helped us." Frank gestured toward the bearded man, who stepped from the shadows to join them. "We guessed where Slovik might take you—but it's too complicated to explain now. Are you all right?"

Tiffany nodded and mustered a quick, brave smile. "Now I am." Her smile faltered. "But Michael's supposed to be back any minute with the other guard. They went to the cabin to get some sleeping bags."

"Then let's get out of here," Frank said, checking the chamber's several exits.

Garth pointed to another dark opening on the far side of the chamber. "That should be the shaft to the entrance behind the cabin."

"I'll get the flashlights and rope," Joe said. He darted into the tunnel they had just come through.

Frank picked up the oil lamp. "Joe can catch up," he told Garth and Tiffany. "I don't want to be around when this guy wakes up."

Quickly Frank led the others to the shaft and stepped inside, lighting the way with the kerosene lamp. He had gone barely ten feet when a bright light beamed out of the darkness ahead of him.

"Put your hands in the air!" a stern voice ordered.

Frank froze. With a sinking heart he realized it wasn't the police.

It was Michael Slovik. Behind him stood the second henchman, loaded down with bedrolls.

"Get those hands up now! Or I'll shoot!" Slovik shouted.

Frank set the lantern on the ground and raised his arms.

Slovik and his companion stepped into the circle of light. Frank's eyes rested on the handgun in the young kidnapper's hand. "All right—back up slowly against the wall," Slovik ordered. Reluctantly Tiffany, Garth, and Frank obeyed.

"Where's your clever brother?" Slovik snarled. "Could he be hiding around here somewhere?"

Frank shook his head. "No, Slovik. He went to get the police. They'll be here any minute. You might as well give up now because—"

"Well, in that case, I hope you brought the computer disks with you," Slovik interrupted. He began pacing back and forth in front of his three prisoners.

"Not a chance," Frank said, forcing a laugh.

Slovik stopped in front of him and gave him a hard, cold stare. "For the sake of efficiency, I'm even willing to pay you for them."

"Don't do it! You know he'll use the formula to murder innocent people," Garth spat out.

Slovik gave the activist a surprised look. "You figured it out? Very good." He turned back to Frank. "It's a terrible problem, you know. International treaties make it very difficult for certain governments to buy nerve gas. And with the spy satellites always watching, it's almost impossible to manufacture it without factories being spotted. But if you have a simple agricultural product—a weed killer, for example—that with just a few simple alterations can be transformed into a lethal weapon . . ." Slovik laughed. "Need I say that it has offered me the possibility of becoming a very rich man?"

"Everything you told me was a lie," Tiffany said bitterly. "That you were a student, that you—"

"Not everything," Slovik said, "but almost everything. I'm a little older than you think. And I have a thriving business as an arms dealer." He turned back and aimed his gun at Frank's stomach. "Now, the disks. Where are they?"

As he was crossing the chamber with the flashlights and ropes, hurrying to catch up with Frank and the others, Joe heard unfamiliar voices echoing ahead. He switched off his light and set the equipment down again. He glanced down to make sure the prone guard had not regained consciousness, then edged toward the tunnel and listened. Soon he heard Slovik's unmistakable laughter.

Joe gripped his darkened flashlight firmly in his fist and gritted his teeth, preparing for his attack. Then he stepped slowly into the tunnel where Slovik held his friends hostage.

In the glow from the oil lantern Joe saw Frank, Tiffany, and Garth lined up against the tunnel wall. Slovik stood facing them. The second guard stood by dutifully, his back to Joe.

Joe crept forward, boldly keeping to the center of the passage. He knew he was safe only until someone turned in his direction.

Tiffany saw him first. Her eyes widened, and she tried to stifle a gasp.

Realizing that he'd been given away, Joe raced forward the last few steps and slammed into the guard's back with his shoulder. The two bedrolls flew out of the man's arms as he stumbled into Michael Slovik.

Frank reacted immediately, kicking at the gun in Slovik's hand. Slovik kept his grip on the weapon. Letting out a terrifying scream, he pulled the trigger.

The bullet exploded into the narrow tunnel, sending shards of rock flying from the ceiling where it hit. Instantly there was a strange, muffled sound like thunder, and a tremor rippled through the mine's rock walls.

With a karate yell Frank kicked Slovik's hand again. This time the gun flew into the darkness deeper inside the mine. As Slovik staggered backward an enormous piece of rock fell from the ceiling, missing Frank by inches.

Tiffany screamed, and Garth yanked her out of the way of more falling rocks. Frank wheeled around in time to see Joe dart to one side, narrowly missing being crushed.

Frank could no longer deny knowing what the sound was, rumbling louder and louder through the mine.

"Get out—now!" he heard Garth yell. "The tunnel's collapsing!"

Chapter

16

MORE ROCKS FELL as Frank heard the wrenching sound of splintering wood. The kerosene lantern suffered a direct hit as a tumbling slab extinguished the flame and plunged the tunnel into darkness.

Frank grabbed Tiffany's arm in one hand and a piece of his brother's jacket in the other. Rocks clattered against his steel helmet. He pulled Tiffany close, wrapped one arm tightly around her, and pushed her head down against his chest to protect her as much as he could. He could hear Garth shouting over the grinding noise of the collapse, and he moved in that direction, pulling Tiffany and Joe with him.

The entire tunnel seemed to collapse behind

them as they raced blindly toward the surface. Frank actually carried Tiffany as he ran. Joe and Garth were close behind him.

Suddenly the air became chilly and fresh, and a square of starry night sky appeared in front of them. Somewhere close by, sirens screamed.

Frank, Joe, Tiffany, and Garth stepped from the mine just as a set of brilliant headlights swept the pines, throwing tall, spindly shadows across the ground. Spinning red and blue lights flickered eerily through the woods. Another set of headlights appeared behind the first, and the sirens died abruptly.

Merilou Parsons was the first up the trail, with two uniformed state troopers behind her. When she saw Garth she rushed into his dirt-streaked arms.

Frank gave Tiffany's shoulders a reassuring squeeze. Joe gasped for air beside them. The three turned and looked back toward the mine shaft, realizing that Slovik and his men hadn't made it out. In the searing white beams of the troopers' lights, only a thick cloud of black dust billowed from the rocks that filled the opening of the old mine.

Several days later Joe woke to the sun shining in his eyes through the glass door of the Gentles' guest room. He sat up and stretched lazily, noticing that Frank was already gone. Delicious smells and cheerful conversation floated into the room from the hallway. Following his nose, Joe wrapped himself in a bathrobe and wandered into the kitchen.

Fenton and Laura Hardy, Aunt Gertrude, Garth Hudson, and Merilou Parsons were crowded around the kitchen table watching a flour-spattered Tiffany Gentle roll out an enormous ball of pastry. Behind them Frank was pouring himself a glass of orange juice while Tiffany's tall, businesslike aunt Elaine jotted down an emergency grocery list.

"Happy Thanksgiving, lazybones," Laura Hardy said to her son with a smile. "Did you know that it's nearly noon? Our guests are already here, and you're late for Tiffany's pastry-making demonstration. She just finished showing us how to mix the butter into the dough with your fingers so you'll know the consistency's right."

"Sorry I missed it," Joe mumbled, joining his brother by the pitcher of orange juice. "What smells so good in here?"

"Turkey, silly." Tiffany's aunt Elaine peered at Joe over her spectacles. "The bird's always the first thing to go in the oven. This may be an impromptu late Thanksgiving, but we can still follow the rules."

"Great. I think it's great we could all get together," Joe said, winking at his aunt across the room. Aunt Gertrude winked back and tossed Joe a salute.

When Fenton's work in Kazakhstan had ended unexpectedly early, the older Hardys decided to fly to Flagstaff to attend Dr. Gentle's funeral and then surprise the younger generation with an old-fashioned—although late—Thanksgiving feast. Tiffany's aunt had been glad to help with the arrangements, and when Tiffany invited Garth and Merilou they insisted on helping cook.

As the pie-baking demonstration continued Fenton slipped away to join his sons by the kitchen counter. "I haven't had a chance to say this to you before, boys," he told them in a low, confidential voice, "but I want you to know I think you both did a terrific job here. Sam never doubted you, either. He was so sure you'd be successful he left you a letter with those computer disks."

Joe grinned and nodded. "I have to admit, it was a surprise finding a package hidden in a remote canyon in the middle of nowhere with our names written on it."

"And the letter to Tiffany cleared up a lot of things, too," Frank said.

Joe recalled the moment a couple of days earlier when the Hardys had finally had time to examine the box Dr. Gentle had hidden in Wolf's Tooth Canyon. Inside they found two letters— Dr. Gentle's legacy in the event of his death.

The letter to Frank and Joe began, "If you are reading this, then you've followed the petroglyph clues I left. . . ."

The letter had gone on to explain something that had puzzled the Hardys—why Dr. Gentle had ignored Garth Hudson's warning. Gentle had taken Hudson's information to Sholdice, who had been a friend and colleague for years. Sholdice had ridiculed the accusations and fired Hudson. But as work on the project continued Gentle began to realize that Hudson was right.

"As it turns out, that's why Dr. Gentle invited us out here," Frank said to his father. "He wanted our help in gathering evidence to give to the authorities."

"But then he overheard a meeting between Slovik and Sholdice in Sholdice's office," Joe added.

Fenton nodded. "Sam knew he didn't have any more time. The work on the formula was finished, and he knew Sholdice was ready to turn it over to Slovik. He couldn't wait even another day, so he hid the disks and trusted that he'd be able to recover them—or, in case of his death, that you were good enough detectives to find it. And you were," he added proudly.

"Talk about good luck for bad guys, though," Joe complained. "They dragged Slovik and his buddies out of that mine collapse yesterday, injured but alive. If Slovik had gotten away with his scheme, thousands of innocent people might have been killed.''

"Yes, but when he's out of the hospital he's going straight to prison," Frank pointed out. "Probably for the rest of his life."

"I hope so," Joe said.

"What's going on over here? Are you guys cooking up another conspiracy theory?" Garth Hudson slipped past them to get a bowl out of the refrigerator.

"We were just reviewing what's happened over the past week," Frank told him as Merilou joined them. "So much has happened—remember, not so long ago we thought *you* were the enemy!"

Garth shot an amused glance at Frank's father. "I'm glad I've been cleared," he told them. "But I wish Sam Gentle were with us."

"Garth, you were pretty rough out there as an demonstrator," Joe said. "But I really admire you for standing up for what you believed in, even with the whole world turned against you."

Merilou smiled at Garth. "Do you hear that, Garth? And you thought no one was listening."

The bearded man smiled self-consciously. "I was a little extreme sometimes. I plan to stay involved in the Anti-War Alliance—but the cause isn't quite as urgent now, thank goodness."

Frank nodded. "Look," he said, "Tiffany's pie crust is headed for the oven!"

Holding two pie pans aloft, Tiffany maneuvered among her guests to put the crust in to brown. As her audience applauded she closed the oven door with a satisfying thunk and announced with great satisfaction, "Now all we do is wait ten minutes and start worrying about the filling."

As the group milled about the kitchen, trading stories and generally getting in one another's way, Frank and Joe found themselves pushed back near the kitchen table with Tiffany.

"Ah—there you are," she said to the brothers, with a wide smile. "I've been meaning to ask you—are you sure you have to fly home tonight?"

"It's time we got back," Frank told her apologetically. "Besides, you'll be at your aunt's in Phoenix. You don't need us cluttering up your house."

Tiffany chuckled and glanced shyly from Frank to Joe. "I want to thank you for all your help," she said. "I wouldn't have survived this without you."

"Sure you would have," Joe replied. "You're a fighter."

For a second Tiffany's smile faltered. "Yeah, right. Like the way I fought with my dad for the last year or so. He really turned out to be a hero, didn't he? I mean, in the end, standing up for what he believed in.''

"Sam was a good man," Fenton said.

Tiffany nodded. "He left that letter for me in case something happened to him—just to let me know that he loved me and believed in me.'' A hint of her former smile returned to her lips. "He even said there was nothing to forgive.''

She turned to Frank and Joe. "I sure am glad you didn't pay any attention to that phone call telling you not to come.''

Joe laughed. "You know us, Tiffany. Calls like that only egg us on.''

"I have to admit, though—this trip to Arizona turned out a lot different than we expected,'' Frank said, shaking his head.

"You should come back in the summer,'' Tiffany told them. "Next time I'll show you guys that there's a lot more to do around Flagstaff than chase after criminals and a mixed-up girl.''

Joe grinned at her. "Well, there's an open invitation for a mixed-up girl to visit Frank and me in Bayport. Any takers?''

"Wild horses couldn't stop me, Joe.'' Tiffany's smile broadened. She pushed back a strand of hair with a floury hand. "I warn you, though, my middle name is Trouble.''

Joe and Frank exchanged amused glances. "Any time, Tiffany Gentle,'' Joe said. "Your kind of trouble is what we live for!''

Frank and Joe's next case:

The Hardys have come to an environmental conference in New York City at the invitation of their friend Ed Yanomama, son of a Venezuelan tribal chief. But in his struggle to save the earth, Ed may end up losing his freedom. Businessman Roger O'Neill, a notorious exploiter of the rain forest, has been kidnapped in Venezuela, and the FBI has put the finger on Ed!

Convinced that Ed has been framed, Frank and Joe head for the jungles of South America. Even as they face blood-hungry bats, flesh-eating ants, and razor-toothed piranha, the boys discover that no animal is more vicious than man. Drawn into conflict with ruthless cattle barons and violent revolutionaries, they cut through a forest of lies toward a truth as shocking as it is deadly . . . in *Poisoned Paradise,* Case #82 in The Hardy Boys Casefiles™.